Julie's Joy

By Jill Dewhurst

Marian,
May you find joy in
God's redeeming love.

Jill M Dewhurst
Isaiah 43:1

ISBN 978-0-9995228-0-6

Dedication

All praise and glory belong to my
loving God and Savior
Who made redeeming love and
true joy possible in the first place.

Table of Contents

Chapter 1
Coming Home

Emma Taylor stepped out her front door and onto her porch. She hadn't been able to smile very much since Daniel's death, but she was smiling today. The telegram in her hand seemed to signify new beginnings. The day was sunny with a warm summer breeze gently blowing the fragrance of her rose bushes toward her. She wore a light blue cotton dress on her petite frame, and her light brown hair was softly pulled up into a bun, giving a matronly look to her thirty-four years.

As she took in the view of her ranch around her, she could see all six of her boys hard at work. Well, they weren't really boys anymore, though the oldest two were just barely out of their teenage years. Her boys were turning into men, and she couldn't be more proud of them. What an eclectic group of brothers they were! The one thing they all had in common was the tragedy of losing their families, for they had all come to her and Daniel as orphans. Now, since Daniel's passing, she, too, understood that loss. How she and Daniel had loved these boys God had sent them! Thankfully, being a young widow didn't mean she had to stop being Mama.

Those boys had seen her through the valley of Daniel's death. A few weeks ago, she had started to see a glimmer of light on the horizon, but today sunlight finally made it back to her heart. Julie was coming home.

"Buck," Emma called to her second oldest, "would you drive me to town, please?"

Buck nodded and walked to the barn to ready the team. Tim strode across to the buckboard, "Emma, it's my turn to go to town."

"I need Buck this time, but the next turn will be yours."

"Okay, Emma," Tim replied, wearing a disappointed frown, but knowing better than to argue.

A few minutes later, Buck climbed up beside Emma and clucked to the horses, sending them on a gentle trot toward town.

Emma looked over at Buck. "Are you wondering why I asked you to drive me when it was Tim's turn to make the trip to town?"

"Yes."

Emma smiled at Buck's short answer. "This isn't an ordinary trip to town. I received a telegram a few days ago that my niece is coming in from the East on the morning stage. Tim might be the fastest driver but at the expense of hitting every pothole along the way. Not a very nice 'welcome home' to be jostled so much. You're my best driver. And I know I can trust you, of all people, not to be quick to judge appearances."

"Will she be quick to judge me?"

"She won't even notice the color of your skin."

Knowing the rest of the ride to town would be in silence, Emma let her mind wander to Buck's first few months at the ranch.

Buck embraced his new culture one small step at a time. His buckskin was put away first as he adopted the clothing of his new brothers. Then boots replaced his moccasins. The final step of his transformation came one Saturday night. He knocked on the front door of the ranch house, and Daniel opened it. Buck asked, "May I speak to Emma, please?"

"Certainly. Come on in." He stepped aside so Buck could enter. "Emma, Buck is here to see you."

Emma came down the stairs with mending in her hands. "Hi, Buck, what can I do for you?"

"Would you cut my hair into the short style of my brothers?"

Emma looked at the two long braids he wore. "I wouldn't mind cutting your hair, but are you sure?"

"Yes. It is time."

"Then come on into the kitchen and have a seat on the stool."

He sat as instructed and began unbraiding his hair. Emma was struck with the realization that his hair was even longer than hers. She understood what a big decision this had been for him. With practiced hands, she removed his long tresses, parted his hair on the left, and tapered it short over his ears and in the back. His thick hair seemed to want to feather perfectly, as if he had styled his hair that way his entire life.

When she finished, she moved to face him. "My, but you look handsome."

With nothing more than a smile and "Thank you, Emma," he rose and exited the way he had come, leaving a small mountain of hair lying on the floor.

Once the front door clicked closed, she observed to Daniel, "That boy of ours never does anything without thinking it through first, but when he makes up his mind, he will not quit until he sees it to the end."

Daniel nodded and laughed quietly, "Yes, his actions are thoughtful and deliberate. I just wish he would rub off on Tim a bit more."

Emma and Buck arrived in town just as folks were gathering to meet the incoming stage, and they ambled over to join the group.

They had their eyes fixed on the stagecoach door. The first to exit was a stately elderly man in a suit who turned to assist a woman dressed in finest fashion. Her face wore a snobbish expression and a scowl. Buck glanced at Emma, glad that she made no sign of recognition. Next came a rather simply dressed, portly girl. Buck still saw no move from Emma.

Finally, the brim of a hat appeared. Beneath it were dark brown curls that framed a beautiful face of ivory skin, smiling brown eyes, a thin nose, and lips parted in a smile. The young woman was dressed in a gray-blue suit, the jacket of which had slightly puffed sleeves and a thin, flat collar. Her blouse had a high neckline with a small cameo broach pinned in the center. The matching skirt was tea-length, flaring from a petite waist to a full hem, long enough to be elegant, but short enough to be practical on the dusty streets. Her smile was so sweet and genuine as she accepted the hand of the stagecoach driver who was helping her down the steps. Something in her gaze, however, wasn't quite right. Before Buck could determine what was amiss, Emma declared, "There she is!"

As soon as Julie's feet touched solid ground, Emma was right there to wrap Julie in her arms. "Julie, how wonderful to see you again! I have missed you!"

"I'm so happy to be back home where I belong."

"Buck, this is my niece, Julie Peterson. Julie, I'd like you to meet Buck Matthews, one of my ranch hands." Emma had nearly called him "one of her boys," but she had resolved to refer to them as "ranch hands" in town as they were now growing into men.

10

Julie extended her right hand for a handshake. "It's a pleasure to meet you, Mr. Matthews."

Buck suddenly realized the reason for Julie's unfocused gaze and understood Emma's comment about her not noticing his skin. Julie was blind.

With a sideways glance at Emma, Buck stepped forward to shake the offered hand. "The pleasure is mine. Do please call me Buck. May I get your things?"

"That would be most kind, thank you. I have a suitcase and a small trunk." Buck excused himself to get Julie's baggage and take it to the wagon.

Emma turned to Julie, "You look stiff. Would you like to take a stroll around town before we head to the ranch?"

"You read my mind. I would love to stretch my legs a bit."

Emma wrapped Julie's hand around her left arm and started walking toward the boardwalk. Emma interjected, "Three steps up."

"Thank you, Emma. You remembered." They continued slowly down the boardwalk, passing the barber and the dressmaker.

Buck joined them just as Sheriff Will Stewart came up to Emma. "Emma, I need to speak to you right away."

Gesturing to the lady on her arm, Emma replied, "Good morning, Will, do you remember my niece Julie? She just arrived on the stage."

"Hello, Julie. I am sorry to interrupt, but it's important."

"Emma, Will sounds urgent. Please go. I'll be all right."

Emma turned to Buck. "Would you mind taking my place? We can meet at the wagon in a few minutes."

"That'll be fine. Is there anything I should know?"

"Just offer your arm, warn her of upcoming stairs, and don't run her into anything. Right, Will?"

"Very funny," he replied. The sheriff extended his hand to Emma as Buck stepped toward Julie.

"Shall we?" He lifted Julie's hand and gently laid it on his arm before they continued strolling down the boardwalk.

Julie was still smiling from the memory. "I had almost forgotten. Not long before I left for the East, the church hosted a dance social. Will was new in town, and he attended to meet the townsfolk. Emma introduced our family, and not realizing she was married, he was completely smitten with her. He danced with me, hoping to cut in when Daniel stopped dancing with Emma. Of course, Daniel wasn't about to let Emma go, but Will was distracted nonetheless. He didn't realize his lack of focus until he ran me right into the barn's support beam. I may still have a scar from that one. He felt awful, then even more so when he learned that Emma was married. I don't think Emma will ever let him live that down." As she told her story, she couldn't help her soft laughter, and Buck relaxed a bit.

"Where are we now?" Julie inquired.

"In front of the general store."

"Is there anything interesting in the window display?" They paused for a moment.

"A saddle."

"Describe it."

"There are scroll patterns etched into the leather."

Julie smiled at his concise description. "It sounds beautiful, though I would have thought you would prefer riding bareback."

Buck raised an eyebrow at her comment. They continued walking, strolling past the sheriff's office and the telegraph office.

Suddenly, Buck stiffened. Julie whispered, "What's wrong?"

"Trouble. Stay close."

Three gruff, ill-mannered men stepped out in front of Buck and Julie. The first man jeered, "Well, would'ya look at that, the prettiest lady in town is walking with the likes of him." Laughter erupted from the trio.

Then the second man chimed in, "Hey, I think she's blind. Bet she doesn't know who she's walking with."

Julie smiled to the first man. "Thank you for your compliment." Then to the second man, "Sir, I know exactly with whom I am walking. Thankfully, it doesn't take good eyes to recognize a man of impeccable character. If you would now excuse us please . . . "

The silenced men parted so they could pass.

A few steps later, Buck asked, "Do you really know whom you're walking with?"

"Well, I think I have a pretty good idea, anyway."

Buck's interest was piqued, "All right, who am I?"

"You must be a man of integrity and good character. Emma mentioned in a recent letter that she was glad she hadn't needed to hire any hands since Daniel died, and he was an excellent judge of character. And she wouldn't hand me off to walk with someone she didn't trust. Besides, I could feel you tense when those men attacked your honor, but you held your tongue. And, unless I miss my guess, you are either Sioux or Kiowa. Between the two, I'd say Kiowa."

Buck stopped and stood in stunned silence for a moment, then commented, "Impressive. How did you know?"

"First, Emma introduced you as Buck Matthews. Though Matthews is not an Indian surname and Buck could be a nickname, I would think it unlikely that one would keep the name Buck in the presence of such anti-Indian sentiment unless it was his given name. Second, your walking gait is smooth and quiet, not like the loud, clomping step of most cowboys. As for your tribe, your accent and the camber of your voice gave you away."

"I truly am impressed, but I must admit that you are only half right."

"How so?"

"My mother was Kiowa, but the man who took her to wife was not."

"But you were raised Kiowa?"

"Yes."

"Would you speak to me in Kiowa?"

Buck replied in Kiowa, *"I can, but you would not understand my words."*

Julie responded in Kiowa, *"You might be surprised how much I understand."* Buck again gazed at her in stunned silence. Julie smiled, "I have missed hearing the tongue of my people, for I grew up with the Kiowa, too, but that's a story for another time. We should probably be getting back to the wagon."

Buck guided her back up the street. "Here is the wagon, and Emma is coming with Will. The step up is a bit tricky. Let me help you." Without waiting for an answer from Julie, he lifted her in his arms and set her gently on the wagon seat, then circled behind the wagon and stepped aside as Will held out his hand to help Emma climb in and sit beside Julie. Buck sat on the end by Emma, and they departed.

On the way to the ranch, Emma and Julie chatted while Buck silently drove the team. Emma inquired, "Did you have a good walk?"

"Yes, it felt wonderful to stretch my legs a bit after the cramped stagecoach, and Buck and I learned we have some things in common."

"Oh? I've always thought of Buck as a man of few words."

"He still is. You just have to listen for answers in what he doesn't say."

Emma looked over at Buck, who was driving the team and wearing a contented smile. "I see."

"How was your conversation with Will? He seemed concerned. Is everything okay?"

"Yes, I think so. A band of cattle rustlers was reported to be headed this direction, so Will has asked us to stay near the Rugged Cross Ranch and be on alert for the next few days."

"Do you think it's a serious threat, or was he being overprotective?"

"I'm not sure, really, but we'll be extra careful anyway."

As Buck brought the buckboard to a stop in front of the ranch house, he leaned forward to speak his first words of the return trip. "Julie, wait there, and I'll help you down."

Emma turned to Julie and whispered softly, "I'll come around and wait for you."

Buck dismounted and extended a hand to help Emma down before he circled behind the buckboard to where Julie was sitting. "Stand and face me, then extend your arms." Julie smiled and did as instructed. Buck took her hands, placed them on his shoulders, and placed his hands around her waist. "There is a short lip to the side of the wagon, and the wheel extends up a bit. Jump up and lift your heels to clear them." She did so and found herself lifted up and over, and her feet were set gently on solid ground. Buck lingered just a moment, gazing at this beautiful young lady with a sweet smile and easy laugh. Then he caught himself and released her waist.

"Thank you."

"You are welcome." Buck glanced over at Emma, who was looking his direction with one eyebrow slightly raised. To avoid her gaze, he simply asked, "Emma, where should I take her luggage?"

"The first bedroom at the top of the stairs. Thank you, Buck. When you finish, would you ask James to come to the house?" Buck nodded his assent.

While he went back to retrieve Julie's things, Emma came up beside Julie and guided her to the house. "Five steps up."

As Buck reached for Julie's suitcase, his gaze returned once more to the young lady gracefully ascending the front steps with Emma. He wondered for a moment how a blind girl could see him so well. Then, with an unconscious smile, he resumed his task.

In the ranch house, Emma led Julie to a chair at the kitchen table and began preparing sandwiches for lunch. "You look tired."

"Yes, I do feel tired. I am amazed how weary one can become riding in a stagecoach for days on end."

"After lunch, I'll help you get settled. You should consider turning in early tonight."

"Emma, you are so thoughtful. I may take you up on your offer tonight, but starting tomorrow, I no longer wish to be pampered. Give me work to do. My desire is to be a blessing and a help to you."

"All right. What kinds of things are you comfortable doing?" Emma inquired.

Julie smiled, "Well, I can perform nearly any task, as long as it does not include a knife or a fire." Emma laughed with her.

A knock sounded on the front door, and Emma rose to open it, stepping aside for James to enter. "Come on in. We need to discuss some news from the sheriff."

James stepped toward the kitchen and noticed the young lady sitting there. "Julie?"

Hearing her name, Julie stood and turned toward the sound. "James, is that you?"

"Yes. When did you get here?" James asked.

"Emma and Buck just brought me home from the morning stage."

"So you're here to stay, then?"

"Yes, I am," she replied confidently.

James stepped up to Julie and extended his arms before he remembered she couldn't see him. "May I give you a hug?"

"Sure."

James gave her a brief brotherly hug and whispered, "Welcome home."

When James released Julie, Emma instructed, "James, have a seat, and I'll get you a cup of coffee."

James sat and resumed his focus as foreman of the ranch. "What did Will have to say?"

"Reports say the Lawton gang is headed this general direction. For the next few days, I need you to set up a rotation to check the herd and the ranch perimeter around the clock."

"I'll make sure the boys pack their rifles and carry their revolvers, just in case." James added. After Emma and James discussed more detailed plans, James left to meet with his brothers.

Emma picked up the cup of tea before her and remembered back to when James first joined her family.

Emma and her husband Daniel had come West as newlyweds and claimed this land to homestead their ranch on acreage that would one day be part of northeastern Oklahoma. They worked hard, knowing that some dreams come only through sweat and tears. As their cattle ranch finally began to be self-sustainable, they needed help to grow.

About the only dream that hadn't yet come true was the one for children. God had not yet answered that prayer. Then one afternoon, Daniel met James McAllister, a boy looking for work. His entire family had been killed in an Indian raid while he was at a neighboring farm on an errand. Though only fourteen, James was tall and strong, with ranch experience and a determination not often found in one so young. Daniel was immediately drawn to this young man, and after speaking to Emma and imploring God for wisdom, he hired James as their first ranch hand. James quickly proved himself to be dependable, hard-working, and quite knowledgeable about horses and cattle. To Daniel, James was like a son, and Daniel sought to teach him not only ranching but his faith as well.

Now James served as the foreman for the ranch. Though Emma could not have imagined depending on anyone the way she had depended on Daniel, James had earned her trust, expertly delegating the ranch's daily responsibilities. Emma considered herself blessed to call him her son.

Buck was standing by his bunk when James came into the bunkhouse. James announced to Tim, who was sitting at the table having lunch, "Now I know why Emma asked for Buck."

"Why?"

"They went to pick up Emma's niece Julie from the stage."

"I could have gotten them home faster."

"Yes, but you'd have rattled her bones getting them here in record time. Emma knows Buck is the best driver of all of us."

"Hmph."

Jacob asked, "When do the rest of us get to meet her?"

"She looked pretty tired, but I'm sure you'll see her around the ranch house tomorrow. Emma had planned dinner for tonight, but something's come up. I'll invite them to join us for Sunday dinner instead. We need to discuss around-the-clock shifts for the next few days." James explained the sheriff's report, and Jacob and Luke left to take the first shift.

James walked over to where Buck was standing. "Julie stayed here at the ranch for a few months before Tim arrived. She's a sweet girl." He noticed the relaxed smile on Buck's face as he packed his saddlebag for the afternoon ride. "And pretty, too."

Buck looked over at James and answered only with a smile.

"Ahh, I see you noticed. Well, see that you keep your mind on your work today."

James needn't have worried. Buck's usual hard work doubled in intensity that afternoon, making James ponder, "Hmm. I wonder if her being here might just be good for that brother of mine."

Chapter 2
The Homestead

The next morning dawned clear and bright, with a soft breeze blowing the smell of fresh cut hay from the side field to where Julie was sitting on the front porch, reading her Braille Bible. She was comfortably dressed in a pink cotton dress with a white apron, and the brown hair that cascaded down her back in soft curls was pulled together with a matching pink ribbon. Her hands paused when she heard quiet footsteps as Buck approached. "Good morning, Buck."

Buck was a bit surprised that she knew he was there and who he was, but his thoughts recovered quickly. "A day this nice should not be wasted on the porch. Would you take a walk with me?"

"What a lovely invitation! I'd enjoy a tour of the homestead to help me get my bearings again." Julie stood, and Buck placed her hand on his arm and guided her down the porch steps. Their walk continued side by side while they toured the bunkhouse, chicken coop, and bunny hutch, rounding all of the immediate ranch dwellings except the barn and corral.

During their walk, Buck ventured, "May I ask how you came to live with the Kiowa?"

"Hmmm . . . I should probably start at the beginning. Emma is my dad's youngest sister. To me, she was more like a big sister than an aunt. When Daniel moved to our town and became part of our church family, he became part of our family, too. Mom and Dad saw how he lived his faith in the midst of trials, and we saw his love for Emma. Those two were destined to marry. When Daniel announced that he and Emma were heading west, no one was surprised. We all missed them terribly. Dad, who had always proclaimed himself a city man, began talking more of the West. With each passing letter from Daniel, his enthusiasm grew. One year after Daniel and Emma left, Dad announced that we were going to head west to homestead near them and help on their ranch.

"When I was nine years old, my family joined a wagon train heading west. Dad's enthusiasm about homesteading land and beginning a new life was contagious. We were all excited, undaunted by storms, heat, or sickness. With each passing day, we were getting closer to our dream.

"Just two weeks before my tenth birthday, our dream was shattered when the wagon master sounded the alert. Our train was being ambushed. The last thing I remember was seeing a band of Indians shouting with their spears raised, racing toward us on horseback."

"Not long after their raid, a Kiowa hunting party spotted the smoke from the charred remains of our wagons. When they arrived, they discovered everything had been pillaged and everyone else in our party, including my parents and my older sister, had been killed and scalped. The Kiowa always suspected the Arapaho, though they didn't know for sure. One of the braves heard a moan and found me unconscious under a piece of crate in a small depression in the ground. The brave brought me back to his village. Apparently, I had quite a lump on my head, but never knew if I fainted and bumped my head in the fall or if something hit me that knocked me unconscious. Either way, when I awoke, I found myself lying in a tepee in the care of a Kiowa woman.

"The chief had declared that since I alone had been spared by the Great Spirit, I should live with his people. Later I learned that this woman and her husband had never had children, so the chief blessed them with me. As it turns out, God really blessed me with them. This couple had such patience with me as I grieved the loss of my family and adjusted to my new surroundings. They accepted me fully, and loved and cared for me as their daughter. White Feather and Runs Like the Wind became my second mom and dad. They taught me the Kiowa tongue and the ways of their people, yet they made sure I never forgot where I had come from. Every evening, they had me read to them in English from the Bible one of the braves had found in the wreckage. They are still as much my family as Emma." Then she added wistfully, "I wonder if I shall ever meet them again."

Buck asked in Kiowa, *"What is your name?"*

Julie answered, also in Kiowa, *"Desert Rose, for the desert shall rejoice and blossom as the rose."*

"It suits you well. In the villages, I am known as Running Buck."

"Running Buck. I feel honored to now know your name."

Buck's words returned to English. "You said you could see and read. Were you not born blind?"

"No, I was not. I did not lose my sight until I was fifteen."

"Julie!" Emma called from the front porch just as Julie and Buck were rounding the house.

"Here, Emma! Buck was just walking me around the homestead."

"I need your help with something."

"I'll be right there." She turned to Buck. "It feels so good to be needed again. Thank you for the walk."

23

"You're welcome. It's time for me to get back to work, too. I'm riding with Josiah for the afternoon check on the herd." Buck walked with Julie to the front door and opened it for her. "Have a good afternoon."

"You, too."

A few days after Julie came home, James sauntered up to the front porch, where Julie was sitting on the swing. "May I join you?"

"Certainly, James. We haven't had a chance to catch up much yet." After he sat down, she asked, "Are you taller than when I left? Your voice sounds higher than I remember." She laughed, "In altitude, that is, not pitch."

James answered thoughtfully, "I'm not sure. How tall was I then?"

"A couple of inches shorter than Daniel."

James responded with a chuckle, "Then I guess I have grown some. I was looking at him eye to eye before he died. I'm a bit over six feet now."

"Daniel was such an amazing man. I still find it hard to believe that he's really gone. I keep expecting to hear him burst through the door and wrap Emma up in a hug and kiss."

"His passing was hard on all of us. Daniel was a man I was proud to call my father. He mentored me in ranching, and after he led me to faith in Christ, he discipled me in my faith. I so wish to be like him. He had truly become the dad that each one of us boys needed. God used him in all our lives."

Julie nodded then added, "I've been wanting to thank you."

"For what?"

"For being Emma's strength when Daniel died. For quietly taking over the reins of the ranch and keeping everything running smoothly so Emma didn't have to worry. When I couldn't come home, you were an encouragement to me just knowing you were here."

"As the first of us to join the family and the eldest of my new brothers, the responsibility of the ranch naturally fell to me. Not until later did I realize that God had prepared me for that responsibility through Daniel's thorough training. I just hope I've made him proud."

"Daniel was very proud of you. Whenever he wrote to me, he would call all of you his 'boys,' but you he always referred to you as his 'son.' As for being like him, if I didn't know your voice, I'd think you were Daniel. You act just like him."

"How so?"

"You carry yourself with the same quiet strength, with authority that should not be questioned, but with a faith and love for others that tempers your every decision. Even when you handled the threat of the rustlers, I could tell how much your brothers respect you."

"Thank you, Julie, I needed to hear that." He gently set the swing in motion.

Julie inquired, "Your brothers didn't begin arriving until after I left for the East. Was the adjustment difficult for you?"

James added thoughtfully, "Not when Tim and Luke came. Tim was as talkative as Luke was quiet; they seemed to balance each other out. They both joined in as if they had always been part of this family. God had to work a miracle of grace in my heart when Buck arrived, but in him I have found a true brother and friend. Jacob and Josiah instantly became our little brothers as the rest of us took them under wing. Putting us together as brothers was definitely God's plan."

"Do you mind my asking what happened when Buck came to the ranch?"

James replied, "Daniel believed in pursuing peace with his neighbors, even his Indian ones. When the nomadic Indian villages would settle within a day's ride, Daniel would take a small group of friends from town to meet the chief and extend the olive branch of peace. That was all well and good on Daniel's time, but I wanted no part of it. I knew in my heart that God loved the Indians just as much as He loved me, but I struggled to believe it. The Indians had slaughtered my parents and brother and sisters. The Indians had even killed your family. I had tried more than once to talk to God about my prejudice, to ask forgiveness, but my struggle continued."

"Then it happened. Daniel returned from one of his peace missions with an Indian dressed in buckskin. He wore long black braids and rode a dark brown and white paint pony. As Daniel introduced the family to Buck Matthews, it began to dawn on me that this Indian was not just here to visit. He was here to stay. The world as I knew it was beginning to tilt."

"I followed Daniel into the barn and asked gruffly, 'Why did you bring him here?'"

"Daniel looked intently into my face, knowing he did not owe me an explanation, but wanting to give me the grace to understand. 'Like you, Buck is an orphan in need of a home. Like you, he has come to faith in Christ. He has heard of the reputation of our ranch and of our faith in the Lord, and I invited him to come so he can also grow in his faith. I understand your struggle, Son, but Buck is your brother in Christ, and he will be your brother here at the ranch. I need you to teach him the ropes around here, not judge him by the color of his skin. Neither he nor his tribe has done anything to hurt you. Go up to the Hill, talk to

God for a bit, and clear your head. Buck will be bunking above you.'"

Julie commented, "Those words remind me so much of Daniel. That's just what he would say."

"I felt as if I'd been punched in the gut, but in the four years I had lived at the ranch, I had learned to trust Daniel as a father. I trudged up to the Hill behind the ranch house to have that talk with God. 'God, you sent your Son to die for the world, not just white men. Please help me to see Buck as You see him. Help me let go of my stubborn pride. Lord, teach me not to just like him, but to love him as the brother he is.'"

"When I came back to the bunkhouse, I walked up to Buck as he was getting settled. 'I did not greet you properly before. I'm James. Welcome to our ranch.' I couldn't quite bring myself to say, 'Welcome to our family.'"

"Buck looked at me eye to eye and said, 'You don't trust me.' There was no judgment in Buck's tone, just the statement of fact."

"I took a deep breath and exhaled slowly. 'I'll be honest with you. My family was killed by Indians, and I've never stood as close to one as I am to you right now. Daniel says you're a brother in Christ, and that's good enough for me. As for trusting you, I'm trying really hard, but I may need some time.'"

"Buck nodded and extended his hand for a white man's handshake. I took this offering of friendship. The next few weeks were rather bumpy. I was frustrated that Buck said so little, when I was trying so hard to communicate. Finally, I realized that Buck's hard work and practiced skill with the horses and cattle were his way of communicating. Though Buck was two years younger, I learned to look up to him in many ways. Ours truly became a bond of brothers."

Julie nodded. "Thank you for sharing that with me."

After a minute, she asked, "Is there a special lady in your life yet?"

James smiled, "Actually, there is. Her name is Emily."

"Emily is a pretty name. Tell me about her."

"She is our pastor's oldest daughter. She is sweet, thoughtful, and quiet, and she has the prettiest smile. She's about your size, but she has blond hair and blue eyes. Since her mom died last year, she has become mom to her younger brother and four younger sisters and has assumed the household responsibilities without a single complaint. I don't think her dad would have made it without her."

"Hmm. She sounds a lot like you."

James smiled, "Yeah, that's what Emma says, too."

"Do you have any plans of starting your own family?"

"Yes, but not yet. Emily's dad still depends too much on her for me to bring her here. I couldn't ask that of either of them."

"So you would live here at the ranch, then?"

"This is my home. I wouldn't dream of living anywhere else. Before Daniel died, he purchased two additional parcels of land, one to the south of the south pasture, and one to the north of the Hill that extends all the way to the river. His purpose was to have enough land that each one of us boys would be able to choose a tract of land and settle right here if we wished."

"That doesn't surprise me. Caring for you boys was very important to Daniel and Emma. You mentioned the Hill. That was Daniel's favorite place to meet with God."

"Yes. He is buried there. The Hill has become a special place for all of us."

Chapter 3
Sunday Dinner at the Bunkhouse

Emma sat down at the kitchen table after breakfast and announced to Julie, "The boys have invited us to dinner at the bunkhouse after church on Sunday."

"How thoughtful! I should be delighted, but I suddenly have butterflies." Julie gave a shaky smile.

Emma reached out to rest her hand on Julie's arm and reassured her, "There's nothing to be nervous about. You've already met all of them. I think they just want to get to know you better."

Sunday morning came, and Julie purposed to put dinner out of her mind so she could fully enjoy worshipping with the family at the little rural church in town. She had attended church regularly near the blind school, of course, but the services tended to be stiff and formal. Her pastor there had preached God's Word, but she had missed Emma's church and the love and acceptance she felt there.

When Emma and Julie descended the front steps of the ranch house, Tim already had the buckboard hitched. Buck walked over to meet them, so he was there to say "Good Morning" and lift Julie onto the buckboard seat as if he did this every day. Then he strode over to his horse, Wind Dancing, mounted, and joined the rest of his brothers on horseback.

Emma sat down next to Julie, "That was thoughtful of Buck.

"Yes, it was," Julie replied with a smile.

The ride to church showcased Tim's reputation as a driver. Julie held on to the seat on one side and Emma on the other, just to keep from flying out of the wagon as he careened around bump after bump in his haste. She was quite relieved when they arrived at the church. Emma glanced over and chuckled at the look on Julie's face. "That's why I didn't have Tim drive you home from the stage."

Julie smiled, "Thank you for that."

As Tim dismounted and helped Emma down, Buck appeared at Julie's side. "Let me help you. Give me your hands." He placed her hands on his shoulders once again. When he had grasped her waist, he asked her to jump and carefully lifted her down to the ground.

"Thank you, Buck."

"You're welcome. Did you survive the ride?"

"Yes, barely." He joined her laughter as he wrapped her right hand around his arm and began guiding her toward the church.

As Emma joined them, Buck spoke quietly to Julie, "Seven steps up." When they arrived at the church's front door, Emma stepped up to Julie's other side to introduce her to their pastor. He and his family had moved to town not long after Julie had left for the East.

"Pastor Kendrick, I'd like you to meet my niece, Julie Peterson. She just moved back home to the ranch after four years away at school."

"Welcome home, Julie. It's very nice to meet you. I hope you will enjoy worshipping with us."

"Thank you, Pastor."

Emma led the way to their usual spot in the third and fourth rows to the right of the center aisle. Buck followed with Julie and guided her into the pew beside Emma. James sat across the aisle next to Emily and her family, and the other brothers filed into the pew behind Buck, Julie, and Emma.

A few minutes later, Pastor Kendrick started the service in prayer, then led the congregation in "Amazing Grace." Julie was delighted to hear Buck's rich baritone next to her soprano. Emma sang melody to her right, while she added a higher harmony. The music lifted her soul and prepared her heart for the sermon. Pastor preached on the parable of the sower and the four soils, an analogy to which these farmers and ranchers could easily relate. Julie evaluated her own heart, and found with joy that hers had been good soil, allowing the Word of God to grow in her heart and begin producing the fruit of the Spirit in her.

After pastor concluded in prayer, he led them in the Doxology and dismissed the congregation. Many people came over to meet Julie; she was a bit overwhelmed trying to remember the names and voices. Emma whispered in her ear, "Relax, you will learn everyone in time." Julie nodded her thanks. James crossed the aisle with Emily.

"Julie, I'd like you to meet my Emily." Julie smiled at his reference to "my" Emily. "Emily, this is Emma's niece."

A soft, musical voice replied, "It's nice to meet you, Julie. I hope we will be friends."

"I would like that very much. Thank you, Emily."

Emma reached for Julie's hand and led her out the door and into the sunshine. Though Julie couldn't see the light, she could feel the warmth on her face. "Seven steps down."

Julie had heard Buck in conversation with some of the other men in the church building and now self-consciously wondered how she would get into the wagon without making a fool out of herself. What she didn't know was that Buck had excused himself and was now coming down the stairs to her. As Emma and Julie finally reached the wagon, Buck was there to ask, "May I help you up?"

Julie released a small sigh of relief and smiled as she replied, "Yes, thank you."

He easily lifted her to the buggy seat and added, "If you make it back to the ranch in one piece, I'll see you there." He offered a hand to Emma, and she climbed in beside Julie.

When Tim climbed up a few minutes later, Emma rested her hand on his arm. "Tim, if you could take the drive a bit more carefully on the way home, we'd be grateful."

"Yes, ma'am," he replied grudgingly.

Tim drove Emma and Julie home without too much jostling. Once again, Buck was there as they arrived and helped Julie down before excusing himself to take care of Wind Dancing. As Tim unhitched the horse, Emma caught Julie by the arm and guided her to the bunkhouse. She spoke to the girl beside her. "Take a deep breath and relax. You will be fine, and they will love you."

"Thanks, Emma, I hope so."

Josiah opened the door for the ladies, and Jacob seated Julie at the near end of the long bench seat on one side of the table. Much ruckus ensued as the hands came in from stabling their horses and worked to set the table and finish cooking the food. Emma leaned toward Julie and whispered, "Are you doing all right?"

Julie smiled hesitantly and answered, "Yes, I'm just feeling a bit helpless, like I should be doing something." Emma gave Julie a gentle squeeze on her shoulder and moved to sit across the table from her. The clatter of plates finally subsided as the food was placed on the table.

Tim stepped over the bench and sat down next to Julie. "I'm sitting by the guest of honor. Buck can't get her all to himself."

Buck sat down next to Emma and said in Kiowa, *"He doesn't know I can see your beautiful face much better from here."* Julie blushed.

Tim smiled at Buck. "Are you saying something bad about me?"

Jacob piped in, "Judging by the look on Julie's face, I'd say Buck was talking to her."

Tim turned to look at Julie. "Wait! You understood him?"

"I did."

"What did he say?" Tim wanted to know.

Julie responded with a teasing smile and nodded toward where she had heard Buck's voice. "If he had wanted you to know, he would have spoken in English."

There was laughter all around, and Tim got an elbow from Luke on his right. Tim addressed the man across from him, "Buck, that's just not fair." Buck just smiled back at him.

As James sat down at the head of the table between Emma and Julie, he added, "On that note, let us pray." All shuffling stopped. Everyone held hands, and James and Tim reached for Julie's hands. "Father in Heaven, thank You for Your many blessings, for this food, for my brothers around this table, for Emma and how she has become the mom we all needed, and for Julie, who reminds us what grace and courage are all about. May she feel loved and welcomed at our table and in our family. In Christ's name we pray, Amen." There were "Amens" all around, followed by the clinking and scraping sounds of food being served.

Tim spoke to Julie, "There's steak, mashed potatoes, green beans, and biscuits. What would you like?"

"A little of each, please."

Tim served her food. Speaking softly, he asked, "How do you know where your food is?"

"Well, unless you misplaced it, it should be right in front of me."

Laughing, Tim tried again, "No, I mean . . ."

Julie, too, was laughing. "I know what you mean; I'm just giving you a hard time. Look at my plate and pretend it's a clock. Tell me where my food is. Like potatoes at 2 o'clock."

"Okay, I get it. Green beans at 2 o'clock, steak at 6 o'clock, biscuit at 9 o'clock, and potatoes at noon. And the guest isn't supposed to give me a hard time."

"I thought everyone was supposed to give you a hard time. I'm just trying to fit in."

Tim responded dryly, "I think it's a conspiracy."

Luke clapped Tim good-naturedly on the shoulder. "See, I told you she was one of us." Conversation around the table was about the sermon, the upcoming church social, the back pasture fence that needed repair, and other ranch business. Julie enjoyed just listening to the voices around her while she ate. She was surprised, and a little disappointed, that she didn't get to hear Buck's voice very much, but she learned much about the other "brothers" around the table.

One morning the following week, Julie was sitting in her chair on the front porch snapping green beans. "Good morning, Tim, Jacob."

"How do you do that?" Tim asked.

"Do what?"

"Know who we are before we even say 'Hi.'"

"What do you think I do while I'm sitting here snapping beans and churning butter? I listen - to your voices and your footsteps. That's how I tell all of you apart."

"So you can tell who we are just by listening to us walk up?" Jacob asked.

"Yes. Though, if more than two of you come at once, it's hard to distinguish the sounds."

"Amazing. I would have guessed we all walk the same way. How do you know who's who?"

"James walks with purpose and authority, and he nearly always wears his spurs that jingle with every step. Tim, you have a confident gait, slow and long-legged, so I'm guessing you're rather tall. Luke has a softer footfall, with very even steps, and he's usually humming, especially around the animals. Jacob, you and Josiah have a very similar gait, relaxed, but deliberate, though Josiah's footfall is a bit lighter and more tentative, and he is apt to whistle. Is he rather shy?"

Jacob seemed impressed. "You've pegged everyone about right, even Josiah."

Tim commented, "The only one she forgot was Buck."

Jacob let out a friendly snicker. "I'm guessing she hasn't forgotten about Buck."

Julie smiled. "If you must know, Buck's is by far the easiest footfall to distinguish. His step is smooth, even, and almost imperceptibly quiet. If he decided to wear moccasins one day, I'd never hear him coming."

Jacob elbowed Tim. "See, told ya."

Chapter 4
Becoming Friends

Buck and Julie fell into a delightful routine of morning walks. When Buck was called away for one reason or another, Julie found she really missed her newfound friend. He seemed very perceptive, especially understanding her avoidance of the horse corral. In truth, what he sensed was her hand unconsciously stiffen around his arm whenever she would hear a horse whinny or when their walk would venture toward the corral. Rather than asking, he would simply turn her another direction and immediately feel her relax again. They had developed an unspoken boundary a good distance from the corral fence.

One morning, Buck finally asked the question he had been wondering for some time. "Why are you so fearful of horses?"

"Did Emma not tell you how I became blind?" Julie asked.

"No. Would you tell me?"

"It's a rather long story."

"I wish to hear it."

"All right." Julie paused to gather her thoughts, then continued, "A few weeks after my fifteenth birthday, the chief's son, Grey Wolf, left a gift for me."

Buck nodded thoughtfully. "He was asking you to be his wife." Buck was surprised what a strong reaction he had to this news.

Julie continued, "Yes. Grey Wolf was a good man, and I would not refuse him. After all, the Kiowa had saved my life, and to marry the chief's son was a great honor. White Feather and Runs Like the Wind were very proud."

"But you were unhappy."

"Unhappy? Not exactly. Disappointed, perhaps. Grey Wolf was a brave warrior who would protect me and provide for my needs, but he already had two wives. I knew he would never love me the way I had always dreamed of being loved - the way I remembered my mom and dad loving each other. Anyway, I needed time to clear my head and pray. If this was to be God's plan for my life, I wanted to have the right heart attitude when I delivered my answer to Grey Wolf. He granted my request to take Nutmeg for a ride. Perhaps he thought it was some strange white man's custom."

Buck smiled at the thought.

"Riding Nutmeg always gave me a new perspective on life. As her name implies, she was a beautiful chestnut. Somehow, I felt a little bit closer to God Himself running through His creation on her back. We were on a familiar trail back to the village when something suddenly spooked her, and she sent me flying through the air. When I landed, the back of my head hit a large flat rock that knocked me unconscious."

"The village knew something was wrong when Nutmeg came back alone, wild with fright. Grey Wolf and two other braves found me and returned me to White Feather. When I awoke, my world was black, and I was terrified. White Feather had such patience with me as I learned to live in my new world. The chief forbade me from riding again, saying this was a sign from the Great Spirit. His son, too, saw this as a sign and released me from the betrothal."

"When even the most experienced horsemen could not calm Nutmeg, the Chief had her put down, and her foal Cinnamon was sold to a neighboring village. Learning of Nutmeg's death broke my heart."

"A few months later, a small party of white men came from a nearby town to establish peace with Chief Soaring Eagle. One of those men was Daniel. When he saw me and asked the Chief about me, he discovered that I was indeed part of the family Emma had lost in the wagon train massacre five years earlier. As you can imagine, I had grown up and tanned quite a bit since he had seen me six years before. Because family was very important to Chief Soaring Eagle, I was reunited with Emma and Daniel."

"The transition was not easy. After so many years, I was finally with my dad's family, yet I couldn't even see them. Being blind was frustrating beyond words. I felt lost and helpless. I knew God had a perfect plan for me, but I had to learn to trust Him. Emma was my constant encourager as I waited for Him to guide me."

"After I was with them for about three months, Emma sent a couple of telegrams East and learned of an institute for the blind. We prayed and had peace that I should go. Emma traveled East with me to get me settled. When I took the oral entrance examination, I was awarded a four-year scholarship, confirming that God was indeed with me. I finished my fourth year and graduated just two weeks before I stepped off the stagecoach and into Emma's arms again."

"I have not ridden a horse since the day Nutmeg threw me, and though I had loved horses before, I am terrified of them now."

Buck responded, "Now I understand why. Was Nutmeg a jittery horse?"

"Not at all. She was smart, alert, sure-footed, and agile. I had raised her from a foal, and in many ways, she had become my best friend. I could tell her anything, and she never told a soul. When I rode her, we moved as one. It was as if she could sense exactly what I wanted without my touching her reins. I would have trusted her with my life."

This Buck understood. He felt the same way with his own horse, Wind Dancing. "Perhaps that is part of your fear. You feel she betrayed your trust."

"I've never thought of it that way, but you may be right. I know she would have never thrown me on purpose. Something frightful must have scared her."

Buck's thoughts wandered back to a horse he had trained years ago. Someday he would tell Julie about that sorrel filly.

After walking in silence for a few moments, Julie spoke, "May I ask, what happened to your family?"

"My father was a solitary man who worked his trap line and traded furs. When he came to our village to trade, he met the woman who would become my mother and took her to wife. A year later, I was born. The winter before my third birthday, my father went out to check his traps and was caught in a blizzard. He never came home. When spring came, my mother and I returned to her village. A warrior in our village had pity on my mother and left a gift for her. She accepted the gift, but he never accepted me. Until the day she died, she never stopped loving me, but Daniel was the first true father I ever knew."

"Did the rest of the village accept you as Kiowa?"

"No, not completely. That is why I began spending my time with the animals. God had given me a gift with horses, though I did not know the Giver of my gift until later. Some of the warriors laughed at my gentle touch with the foals until they grew old enough to train. Even as a boy, I could train my horses much more easily than the other men could train theirs. The end result was that my horses were more responsive and less skittish. Mine were the horses they wanted to ride. Eventually, I began to earn the respect of the warriors, though they never really considered me one of them. I was half white, after all."

"How did you come to know the One True Great Spirit?"

Buck smiled. Only one comfortable with Indian customs would give his God that title. Then he turned pensive again. "Not long after I turned fifteen, my mother died of a sickness, and I suddenly felt very isolated. Pouring myself into the horses gave me time to think. If there was a Great Spirit, then He had created me half Kiowa and half white. Perhaps it was time for me to learn more about the white men. I began learning what English I could from visiting traders."

"When a neighboring village offered to buy some of my horses, I took them to make the trade. There I met a Kiowa maiden who spoke English. When I asked how she had learned English, she told me her friend in the village had taught her. As we talked together, I mentioned wishing for an English book to read. She left and returned with a Bible."

"I began studying the words to build my skill in English. Those words pricked my heart, for they told of the Creator who loved me enough to send His Son to die a cruel death as payment for my sin. They told of the triumph over death as He rose again and lives forever, of His gift of salvation to all who would believe, even a man who was half Kiowa and half white. He was offering his gift to me, and I accepted it."

"My desire to grow in my faith seemed thwarted at every turn. Then Daniel and his friends came to the village. Something drew me to him. The more we talked, the more I wanted to be like him. He spoke of the Great Spirit as a friend and father. I told him of the death of my family and my search for the truth. The next morning, he invited me to come back with him and live on his ranch as one of his boys."

"At first, the idea seemed ridiculous. Leave the only home I ever remembered? Live with the white men? 'Pray about it,' Daniel had said. When I did, my halting prayer yielded something amazing. Peace. I walked to his camp just outside the village to give him my answer. I will never forget the look of joy on his face as I told him. I returned to the village only to get my things and my horse, and I never looked back."

"Daniel had the foresight to speak to the Chief before he invited me to come with him, so my relationship with the Chief was unharmed by my decision. That wisdom has continued to bridge the gap between our ranch and the villages with peace."

"How old were you when Daniel brought you here?"

"Sixteen."

"Were you the last of the brothers to join the family?"

"No. Jacob and Josiah came the year after I arrived."

"They are blessed to have you for a brother."

"It is I who am blessed. I am thankful that Daniel found me and brought me to the ranch. Here I am finally home."

Chapter 5
Seeing Faces

Emma and Julie sat at the kitchen table enjoying a cup of hot tea to celebrate being done with laundry for another week. Emma sighed, "Those boys sure do dirty up a lot of clothes in a week. I'm feeling old and tired."

"Tired, I understand, but you certainly don't sound old."

"I'm looking old these days."

"I don't believe it. Let me see your face." Emma leaned in and lifted Julie's hands to her face. Julie's fingertips started at Emma's hairline and studied every detail as they traveled down to her chin.

"See, what did I tell you?"

"You do not look old, though you may have a new line or two around your eyes since Daniel died."

"It's a wonder how well you can see with those hands of yours."

"Unfortunately, there are too many things my hands can't see. I have the heart of an eagle, but my broken wings cannot fly."

"What was that?"

"Oh, just something Buck would say. The words sound better in Kiowa."

"He's special to you isn't he?"

"Every one of the ranch hands is special to me in his own way, but Buck is different. Maybe because we both understand the Kiowa and the white man's worlds. That understanding seems to connect our souls somehow."

"I don't know about connected souls, but I will say that Buck has said more words to you since you came than I've heard from him since he's been on the ranch. And I've never seen that boy smile so much."

"I'd love to be able to see his smile. I do wish I knew what he looked like."

"He's handsome. Of course, all my boys are handsome." A sudden idea struck Emma, "You should ask to see Buck's face."

"Describe the boys for me. What do they look like?"

"You're trying to change the subject, but I'll humor you." She took another sip of tea. "Let's see. James just turned twenty-two. He is just over six feet tall with broad shoulders, thick dark brown hair, and brown eyes. Buck is maybe an inch shorter than James, a bit thinner, too, but probably the strongest of the bunch. He definitely looks Indian, but his features are softer, less angular. He's twenty. Tim is my tallest boy. Why, he must be six-and-a-half feet. He is lanky with sandy blond hair and green eyes. He's nineteen, and I hope he's stopped growing. Trying to keep that boy in pants that fit is a challenge. Luke is seventeen; he is a couple inches shy of six feet with blond hair and the bluest eyes. He is thin but muscular with a boyish face and a handsome smile. Jacob is sixteen, and Josiah is fifteen. They were born brothers and resemble each other a lot. Both have brown wavy hair that always stays unruly, freckles on their noses, and the most adorable dimples when they smile. Jacob's eyes are brown, and he's Luke's height. Josiah has hazel eyes. He's a few inches shorter than Jacob, but I think he might just pass him before he finishes growing."

When Emma paused to lift her teacup once again, Julie asked, "I have heard the stories of how James and Buck came to the ranch, but I don't know anything about the other boys. What brought them here?"

"Well, a couple of months after you left for school, Daniel received a telegram from his cousin. A close friend of his, a lumberjack, had been killed in a logging accident, leaving a fifteen-year-old son with no family. The boy's mother and baby sister had died in childbirth when he was ten, and he had no other siblings. Daniel's cousin and his wife already had five children and had no room for another. Besides, he knew the boy's dream was ranching. Daniel traveled to northern Missouri and brought Timothy O'Brien home with him."

"Tim! I was trying to figure out which brother this was going to be," interrupted Julie.

"Tim was confident, even a bit cocky and impulsive at times, but he had a big heart. I wondered more than once whether the attitude was just a cover-up to hide his vulnerability. He wasn't afraid to speak his mind, though, so no one ever had to wonder what that boy was thinking. His grief was raw and open, but Daniel always knew just what to say to convey God's comfort to his heart. Having James so grounded in his faith by then was a real encouragement to Tim also, for James could truly empathize his loss."

"One month later, Dr. Mason stopped by to see Daniel. A wagon train moving through the north side of town had been exposed to cholera. The sickness spread through the families quickly, and several people died, including one boy's parents and older brother. Luke Hamilton had suddenly become an orphan. Daniel and I agreed that he should ride up with Doc and bring Luke to live with us. Luke didn't say much at first, not that he could get a word in edgewise with James and Tim around, but his eyes . . . Oh, those blue eyes of his spoke volumes. The pain and grief mirrored there broke my heart. At thirteen, he was still as much boy as man. There were times I would just hold him tight and tell him I loved him."

"Daniel felt he couldn't connect with Luke the way he had with the other two, and he spent many nights on the Hill sharing his burden with his Lord. Then early one morning, Daniel found Luke sitting in the hay next to his horse in the barn. He was reading the book of Psalms. That was the moment Daniel knew Luke was going to be okay. For me, that moment came when I caught Luke humming in the barn after he had returned from helping a heifer deliver her first calf. When he heard me, he looked up, and those blue eyes were actually smiling."

"Right away, Daniel noticed Luke's aptitude with the animals. Luke was quiet and gentle, yet he could be firm when necessary. He peppered Doc with questions whenever he visited the ranch and learned quickly what he could apply to the animals in his care. He read everything he could find on veterinary medicine, and Daniel soon entrusted him with the medical needs of our animals."

"Buck was the next of the boys to join our family. A year after Buck's arrival, Daniel and I began to feel that familiar tug, the one that hinted we needed to add to our family once more. So we prayed for God's wisdom and guidance. We didn't want to rush His will, but we didn't want to miss it either. One evening, our pastor came by for an unexpected visit. I welcomed him in, and Daniel rose from the chair to meet him, 'Evening, Pastor. What can we do for you?'"

"'Well, Daniel, I'll get straight to the point. A preacher friend of mine in the next township runs an orphanage that is bursting at the seams. Two of the older boys, brothers actually, have volunteered to leave to make room for the younger ones. Jacob and Josiah Collins are only twelve and thirteen. My friend doesn't think they are old enough to go, but he's at a loss for what to do. He telegrammed me, asking me to pray for wisdom and give my counsel. As I was praying, the Lord kept bringing you to mind. Would you be willing to accept two more boys into your family?'"

"'Pastor, we have been praying about that very thing; we just didn't know who we were praying for.' Looking to me for confirmation, he continued, 'We would be happy to have the two boys come live with us.' Jacob and Josiah arrived a couple of days later, and our family was complete. The boys had already worked through their grief, but they craved the love and acceptance of their new big brothers."

"Jacob was rather out-spoken. He had been the leader of the kids at the orphanage, and I feared he and Tim might clash. Tim surprised me by taking Jacob on a horseback ride. They were gone all afternoon. I never knew what they said to one another, but they returned the best of friends. Of course, it couldn't have hurt that Tim towered over Jacob," Emma added with a laugh.

"Josiah was more of a quiet follower, though he was discerning enough to ask questions when he didn't see the wisdom in what he was asked to do. Luke was the one who took the initiative to mentor Josiah. When I asked Luke about it later, he told me he wanted the Lord to use him in Josiah's life the way the Lord had used Buck in his life. Luke still looks up to Buck, and Josiah still looks up to Luke."

"The way those brothers have become our family could only be the result of God's sovereign hand. Daniel loved his boys, and every one of them found in Daniel a man they could love, trust, and respect as a father." Emma chuckled again, "I had always imagined myself with little girls, and God gave me six boys. Now I wouldn't trade them for all the little girls in the world."

"Spoken like a true Mama," Julie added.

Emma refocused the conversation. "Now back to the topic. You really should ask to see Buck's face."

"Oh, no, I could never do that."

"Why not? You just saw my face, and you saw Daniel's and James' faces when you were here before."

"Buck is Kiowa."

"And . . .?"

Julie explained, "In the Kiowa culture, touching someone's face is very intimate. Only a husband and wife would touch each other's face."

"I think Buck would understand your motive. You should ask him."

"I don't think so."

Emma persisted, "You'll never know unless you ask. Promise me you'll ask. The worst he can say is no."

"You're not going to let this go, are you?"

"Nope."

Julie took a deep breath before responding, "All right, I'll ask him, but I'm still not sure it's the right thing to do."

The next morning Julie sat in her chair on the front porch trying to focus enough to read, when Buck approached and sat in the chair next to her.

"Why are your eyes sad?"

"Am I that transparent?" A soft sigh escaped. "Emma made me promise to ask you something I've been wishing to ask, but the answer may be difficult, and I would never want you upset with me."

"Keep your promise first. Let me take the burden of the answer."

Julie took a deep breath for courage, then spoke hesitantly, "May I . . . May I see your face?"

Buck asked gently, "How?" He leaned forward and rested his elbows on his knees.

Julie's face turned thoughtful. "When my eyes could no longer see, my ears and my hands became my eyes." She gestured to her Braille Bible. "When my fingers feel the raised bumps on the page, my mind sees letters and words in ink on paper, not dots. When I feel a cup, I can see the exact shape and size of the cup and its handle." She bowed her head as if looking down at the hands in her lap.

As understanding dawned on him, Buck spoke, "You are asking to touch my face."

"Yes, and I know the way of the Kiowa would forbid it. If I could see with my eyes, I would certainly never ask such a thing. If you should answer no, I would completely understand." A quiet tear trickled down Julie's cheek.

Buck understood the inner turmoil Julie's simple question had cost her, and his heart yearned to comfort her. "You understand me better than anyone else I have ever known, but you have forgotten one thing. I am Kiowa, but I am also white, and I have chosen to live in the white man's world. I find great joy in seeing your face every day, so I could never deny your wish to 'see' mine." Buck removed his hat, placed it on the table beside him, and knelt on one knee directly in front of where Julie was sitting. With his thumb, he gently wiped away the tear on her cheek and said, "I have touched your face, now you may touch mine."

As he lifted her hands toward his face, Julie whispered, "Are you sure?"

"Yes." He placed her hands so her fingertips were touching his forehead. "What do you see?"

"The forehead of my Kiowa brothers. What color are your eyes?"

"Brown, like yours."

Julie offered the hint of a smile, studying his eyes and cheekbones, nose, and jawline, trying to memorize every detail. Buck couldn't help the smile that emerged.

"Your smile lights your face. How deep is the color of your skin?"

"I have the bronze skin of my mother."

Julie's smile was growing. "Just as I had imagined. Do you have the hair of your mother as well?"

Buck moved Julie's hand to the top of his head to feel the texture of his thick, mostly-straight hair. "Yes, it is the color of ravens."

"Your hair is shorter than I expected."

"I have been wearing the haircut of my brothers for the last few years."

"Thank you," Julie whispered, but as she began to lower her hands back to her lap, Buck brought them to his lips and kissed her fingertips.

"You are most welcome. You may see my face again whenever you wish.

Chapter 6
The Church Social

Early autumn was a busy time in their community. Once haying was done for the season, the tempo on the ranch slowed down a bit as the focus turned to needed repairs and filling the woodshed with firewood for the winter. The cattle still had to be checked and rotated from pasture to pasture until the snows began, but their change in responsibilities allowed some to work double duty at the ranch so others could be free to help the farmers in their church harvest their crops before the first snow. The brothers put in long hours to be a blessing to the farmers around them. Emma and Julie traveled from farm to farm making lunch for the extra workers. Requests for good weather were in everyone's prayers. The bond of community was felt by everyone, so it was fitting that they should celebrate the end of harvest together also. The annual church social was that celebration.

Even after James asked Emily to the social, none of the other boys would ask Julie, supposing Buck would. But he didn't. The time of the social drew nearer, and James asked Buck why he hadn't asked her yet. Buck didn't answer. "I'm sure you have your reasons, but I know one beautiful young lady who will be very disappointed."

As Buck finished repairing a loose board on the side of the house under the window, Emma paused from hanging laundry on the clothesline to corner him. "Buck, why are you afraid to ask Julie to the social?"

"I am not afraid to ask."

"So, why haven't you asked? Every time someone mentions the event, you duck out of the conversation." With gentle concern, she reached out to rest her hand on his arm. "I even heard a rumor that you volunteered to stay here and look after the animals. What is it, Buck?"

Buck paused to look at Emma, then answered slowly. "Julie will be the most beautiful one there, but I cannot bear to watch her dance with another."

"I'm not sure I understand. Why wouldn't you be dancing with her?" Buck looked uncomfortable and swallowed hard. Understanding dawned on Emma. "Oh, Buck, do you not know how to dance?"

"Not the way white men dance."

"Now that I can do something about," she replied with a smile.

Each evening after dinner, Emma met Buck in the barn, away from curious eyes. Emma had never seen Buck act so timid. He never said much, but he always carried himself with a quiet confidence. When she met him in the barn that first night, that confidence had vanished. As she began teaching him how to waltz, she learned that his graceful stride had two left feet. He accidentally stepped on her toes so many times that Emma wondered if he would return the next evening, but it wasn't in Buck's character to quit. He did, however, come to his second lesson in moccasins so he wouldn't injure her toes so much. Once he finally got the pattern of the steps memorized, Emma started humming a waltz tune while they moved, so he could learn the relationship of the movements to the music.

Weeks later, on the night of his last lesson, Emma closed her eyes in order to dance from Julie's perspective, just to be sure she hadn't neglected any special instructions. "Buck, you will need to guide her left hand to your shoulder and take her other hand in yours. Practice." He obeyed. "Good. Now gently guide me across the floor as you dance." Then she added with a chuckle, "And don't run me into anything." As they finished their waltz, Emma declared, "Nicely done. Julie must have a lot of faith and trust in people to be so relaxed when being led around. I must admit the feeling is a bit unnerving. By the way, yesterday at church I overheard a young man ask James if Julie had been asked yet, so I'd advise you to invite her before he does."

The next morning, during his walk with Julie, he ventured, "Has anyone asked you to the church social?"

"No," she answered, disappointment in her voice.

"Would you honor me by allowing me to escort you?"

Julie's face lit in a smile, "Yes."

"Buck?"

"Yes?"

"Thank you for asking."

"You are most welcome."

The night of the event finally came. Emma had left early in the buckboard with James. He dropped her off at the venue to help with the final decorating while he picked up Emily. The other boys rode their horses so Buck could use the buggy. He harnessed the horse before walking up the porch steps to where Julie was waiting on the swing. She was wearing a cream-colored dress with a ruffled collar encircling the modest scoop neckline. The sleeves were three-quarter length with another ruffle around the cuffs. The azure blue sash at her waist was tied into a bow behind her. Her curls were pulled up and decorated with cream ribbons and small flowers. She looked lovely. Buck couldn't help the smile that appeared on his face. "Shall we?" he asked. Julie stood, and Buck led her down to the buggy, again sweeping her in his arms and setting her carefully on the seat before rounding the buggy to climb up the other side.

"Thank you."

"You are welcome."

Julie explained, "Being blind carries many insecurities. One of the worst is climbing in and out of a wagon of any kind. I have embarrassed myself more than once by falling when my foot has missed the foothold or my hem has caught in the wheel. Now I can relax and enjoy the ride."

"Then I shall continue lifting you."

Julie quickly changed the subject, "Is it dark yet?"

Buck smiled at her discomposure, "No, the sun is just beginning to set."

"Is the sky clear or cloudy?"

"Clear. The stars will be out soon."

"The evening sounds beautiful."

"You are the one who is beautiful."

Julie blushed. "Thank you."

They traveled the remaining distance to the social in comfortable silence. When they arrived, he lifted her down, rested her hand on his arm, and escorted her into the barn. The sound of music and the smell of fried chicken met them as they entered and walked over to where the other brothers had congregated.

When Tim saw Julie, he blurted, "Wow, you sure look pretty tonight. Will you save one dance for me?"

Jacob elbowed him in the ribs.

"What?"

"She's on Buck's arm, genius. I'm guessing she'd like to dance with him."

Tim muttered, "I only asked for one dance."

"Yeah, but if you get one dance, then the rest of us would want to get one, too. I know I would," replied Jacob.

"Me, too," chorused Luke and Josiah.

Julie laughed, "I don't think I've ever been so popular. You are all so sweet. Jacob is right, though. Only one of you asked me here tonight, and unless Buck lets you cut in, my dances belong to him."

Pastor Kendrick rang a bell to get everyone's attention, then he opened the event in prayer. After his "Amen," the lead musician announced the first waltz.

Buck looked down at Julie and asked, "May I have this dance?"

With a smile, she replied, "Yes, you may."

He led her to the dance floor, lifted her left hand to his shoulder, and wrapped her other hand in his left as his right hand circled her waist. He glanced up to see Emma standing next to James and Emily. Emma smiled and nodded her encouragement. Buck smiled and returned his gaze to the one in his arms.

Before James led Emily to the dance floor, he leaned toward Emma, "I didn't know Buck could dance."

"He couldn't until a few weeks ago."

"So that's what you've been doing in the barn every night."

Emma just smiled.

"Now that explains everything."

As the first strains of the waltz began, Buck guided Julie with stiff steps that gradually relaxed as the song continued. In truth, he still felt very awkward, but he was willing to endure awkward to be close to Julie. If she noticed he was tense, though, she didn't let on. He let Tim cut in on the fourth dance, then Jacob, Luke, and Josiah each took a turn. Julie glided gracefully and effortlessly across the floor. James approached Buck, "Would you mind one last interruption?"

"I suppose not. Go ahead."

James walked out to the dance floor and cut in for Josiah. "Are you having fun? You dance beautifully by the way."

Smiling up at him, Julie replied, "Yes, I am having fun, and thank you, James. I was starting to wonder where Buck had gone, though."

"He doesn't have to wonder where you are. He hasn't taken his eyes from you all evening."

Julie smiled shyly.

"Do you know why Buck took so long to ask you?"

"No."

"He didn't know how to dance. Emma has been teaching him in the barn every night for the last couple of weeks."

"He learned how to dance just for me? How thoughtful!" Then, laughing, she continued, "Now I know why Emma had to check on the animals every night."

"Buck is not only my brother. He has become a close friend and a man I admire, and I'm very glad he has you for a special friend."

When James met Buck's gaze and nodded to his brother, Buck strode to meet them. "Now I return you to the man you came to dance with. Buck, thanks for letting us all have a turn dancing with Julie." He smiled at Buck and clapped his shoulder in a brotherly gesture before rejoining Emily.

Buck lifted Julie's hands where they belonged, and they danced together again. He felt more relaxed now, and his former look of concentration was replaced by a smile. He wasn't planning to let anyone else cut in for the rest of the evening. Several songs later, the lead musician announced the evening's final waltz.

"Would you dance one more waltz with me?"

"Gladly," she replied.

Buck reached once more for her hands without even needing to think about it. As the music began, they danced together as one, moving smoothly across the floor. He had found his graceful stride once again. Emma looked on from across the room and could not help the smile that appeared. Despite his hesitation before tonight, his confidence had returned, and he didn't run Julie into the barn beam even once.

The next day after dinner, Emma made two cups of tea. She and Julie settled at the kitchen table for a chat.

Emma started the conversation. "James has been sweet on the Pastor's daughter Emily for awhile now. I had just assumed he'd be the first to start a family of his own. Now I must admit that I think Buck will be the first of my boys to marry."

Surprise and disappointment shrouded Julie's heart. "Who is Buck going to marry?"

"Are you kidding? You, of course."

"Me?" Julie was genuinely surprised. "No, Buck wouldn't want to marry me," she insisted. "We just have a lot in common, and he needs a friend."

"I don't mean to be unkind, my dear, but you must be really blind not to notice how Buck cares for you. Of course, you might not realize the change in him since you arrived. He is still far from talkative, but he has opened his heart to you, Julie. I see his easy smile much more frequently, and somehow he finds time each day to wander by the front porch for a walk."

Julie's eyes misted, and Emma laid a gentle hand on Julie's arm. "What is it? Did I say something wrong?"

After taking a shaky breath, Julie explained, "Thanks to my mom's example, I have an ideal of what a wife should be, and I feel so inadequate and helpless being blind. Buck deserves the very best in a wife, and I cannot be it, not blind. Why, I am not even able to adequately cook or clean." Julie reached up to wipe away a wayward tear. "If God blessed Buck and I with children, how could I care for them? No, such thoughts are utterly unfair to Buck. I must not entertain them."

Emma could see both pain and determination in Julie's expression. "Oh, Sweetheart, I had no idea you felt that way. You always seem so graceful and confident. To be honest, I don't think your blindness matters to Buck."

"It matters to me."

If Julie were honest, though, she would realize that her heart was already very much in love with this man she could not see.

Chapter 7
Thanksgiving

Now that harvest was complete, the time had come for winter preparations. Emma and Julie had finished canning and storing the garden fruits and vegetables, and the cellar shelves were lined with neat rows of mason jars and bushel baskets. Josiah tilled the garden, getting the soil ready for its winter rest. The other boys were completing the repairs around the ranch and filling the woodshed with firewood.

With the first snowfall came a change in ranch responsibilities. The cattle would no longer need to be rotated between pastures until the snow thawed in the spring. Now the boys needed to be sure the cattle were regularly supplied with hay. James and Luke hung the ropes from the ranch house to the barn and the bunkhouse that would be the lifeline in the event of a blizzard. The heavy snow didn't usually come until after the first of the year, but being prepared was always wise.

One afternoon in mid-November, the blue sky filled with low, gray clouds. The next morning, everything was blanketed in white. The sun had returned, and the sunlight reflected off the ice crystals in the snow, making the ground sparkle. Buck, all bundled up against the chill of the day, described the scene to Julie as they took their morning walk.

Next week would be Thanksgiving, and Julie had so much to be thankful for this year. As they strolled along in front of the corral, Buck noticed Julie's smile and asked, "What are the thoughts behind that smile?"

"I just realized that this will be my first Thanksgiving holiday since before my family joined the wagon train. I'm just so thankful to have family with which to celebrate my childhood traditions again."

"Didn't you celebrate Thanksgiving at the blind school?" Buck asked.

"No, most of the students would go home for Thanksgiving, leaving me and a couple others to have a quiet and rather lonely weekend. Of course, we didn't celebrate a traditional Thanksgiving in my Kiowa village, either." After a pause, she inquired, "How do you celebrate here at the ranch?"

"After we finish our morning chores, we gather in the ranch house for a big breakfast. Once we help Emma clean up, James gets the turkey in the oven, and we sit around the fireplace and tell stories about what we're thankful for from the last year. When we get hungry, we all help cook Thanksgiving dinner while Emma makes her cranberry sauce."

"Hmm. I wonder where I'll fit in."

"That's easy. You'll be the one we're all thankful for."

Julie blushed. "I meant where I could help."

"You can help me make the mashed potatoes," Buck offered.

"Good. Thank you," Julie replied.

Buck laughed, "You're welcome. Don't forget that James and I will be away from the ranch for the next day or two."

"Yes, I remembered. Where are you going?"

"To hunt a turkey for dinner."

"I'll look forward to your return. I love turkey," Julie teased.

James and Buck left in the middle of the night to be in place in the brush before sunrise. Their patience while braving the chilly temperatures was rewarded with a twenty-pound tom turkey. Buck brought him close with his turkey calls, and James dropped him with one shot. They were home before noon.

James brought the turkey into the ranch house to show Emma.

"Look at that huge tom! Is he the biggest one you've brought home?"

"Maybe. I'm going to lay him on the back porch for a few minutes while I warm up. The temperature really dropped last night. I'm frozen."

"Go ahead. I'll get you some hot coffee."

"Thank you, Emma."

James deposited the tom just outside the kitchen door and returned to cup both hands around a steaming mug of coffee from Emma. He sat down at the kitchen table across from Julie and began sipping the hot liquid.

Emma remarked, "That turkey must have been waiting for you. I don't remember you ever being back home so soon."

"Buck must have been sweet-talking him with his call. The tom just kept strutting closer until I had the perfect shot."

Emma laid her hand on James' shoulder. "Don't minimize your skill, James. You're the best shot of all my boys, maybe even of every boy in the territory. You and Buck make a good team. Speaking of Buck, where is he?"

"He's taking the horses to the barn. He'll be here in few minutes."

About fifteen minutes later, the front door opened and closed, and Julie recognized the soft, even step of the one who entered. She turned to Emma, "May I have another mug of hot coffee, please." Emma handed her the mug, and Julie turned to give it to Buck.

Buck took the coffee from Julie, "Thank you." She jumped when he reached out with icy fingers and took her hand.

"You are half frozen," Julie spoke with concern.

"Come." He led her to the sofa in front of the fireplace where the fire was crackling and sending out its warmth. "If you don't mind, I'd like to visit with you right here today where it is warm."

"I don't mind at all," replied Julie.

James stood up from the kitchen table and addressed Emma, "I think I've finally thawed out a bit. I'll go pluck and clean the turkey and hang him in the smokehouse."

"Thank you, James." He exited the kitchen door.

Julie asked Buck, "Does James take care of the turkey all by himself?"

"Yes, he is rather particular about his turkey. He rather prides himself in taking the bird from living to the plate. He will shoot, dress, smoke, brine, roast, and carve his turkey. Any offers of help will be flatly refused."

"I'm surprised, then, that he lets you come on the hunt."

"He takes me for two reasons. First, my turkey call is better than his. There are advantages to being Kiowa, after all. Second, he knows he can trust me not to touch his turkey. Besides, once the first snowfall of the season comes, we travel in pairs in case we were ever caught in an unexpected snowstorm."

Knowing how Buck's father had died, Julie wondered if Buck had been the one to implement this winter rule, but she thought asking would be insensitive.

The day before Thanksgiving, Emma and Julie were busy making pies. By dinner, three pumpkin and three apple pies were cooled and ready for the following day. The house smelled of delicious cinnamon and nutmeg. Julie could remember her mom often saying that those were her two favorite spices. That memory had inspired her when she named her Indian horses. The spicy smells filling the air reminded Julie of her first home and the fun times her family had shared this time of year.

Thanksgiving Day finally arrived. The brothers were up early, busy doing their morning chores, while Emma and Julie prepared breakfast. One by one, the men entered. Out of respect and remembrance, the place at the head of the table was set but kept empty. That had been Daniel's chair. Julie and Emma sat on either side of the empty chair. After Luke sat down next to Julie, the other brothers took a chair. The only one missing was Buck, and the only remaining chair was at the foot of the table.

Buck's brothers had witnessed him in silent prayer many times, but they understood the influence of his Indian heritage. To Buck, prayer was very personal, between him and God alone.

Jacob spoke to James sitting across from him, "Will you pray since Buck isn't one for praying much in front of others?"

"No, our tradition is that the one at the foot of the table prays. Buck will be all right."

Buck finally entered through the kitchen door. He sat in the remaining chair, held his hands to his brothers on either side and spoke without hesitation, "Let's pray." Everyone around the table held hands, and he began, "My Creator and Lord, this year we have endured great sorrow when You took Daniel to live with You. We have also enjoyed great blessing on the ranch with the cattle and with our good health. Most of all, we are thankful that Julie has come home to the ranch, and I pray she will be a part of my family forever. Thank you for this breakfast that begins our day of Thanksgiving. In my Savior's name, Amen."

Tim whispered to James, "Did you hear him say 'part of my family' instead of 'our family'?"

"What I heard was Buck praying from his heart. Leave him alone," commanded James.

Down the table, a similar conversation was taking place as Luke leaned toward Julie, "He wants you to be a part of his family, huh?"

Julie whispered back, "He might have accidentally used the wrong word."

Luke laughed softly, "If there's one thing I know about Buck, with as few words as he says, nothing is ever said by accident. He's obviously had this conversation with God before."

Thankfully, the attention of the hungry men at the table quickly turned to the food. Luke served Julie, and soon stories and laughter filled the room while they ate.

When the sound of utensils on the plates quieted down, Emma spoke, "All right, boys, time to clean up."

There was a chorus of "Yes, ma'am" followed by the scraping of chair legs as everyone got up to clear their places and clean the kitchen. Julie rose also, pushed in her chair, and carried her plate toward the counter. Tim took her plate, and she moved to the sink to start washing dishes. Emma took her by the arm, "Julie, come and sit. Let the boys do the work today."

"Please let me help them, Emma," Julie begged.

"All right, if you really want to help, go ahead."

"Thank you, Emma." Julie made her way back to the sink and rolled up her sleeves.

Josiah stepped up beside her, "If you wash, I'll rinse."

"Just let me know if I miss a spot," Julie requested.

"And I'll dry," piped up Jacob.

Tim stood to Julie's left, "I've scraped the last plate. They're in a stack here with the silverware and glasses behind. I'll help James finish scouring the pans."

"Thank you, Tim," Julie replied.

Buck reached around Julie to add some more hot water from the kettle to the sink, then he soaked a rag in the soapy water. "I'll wipe the table down and add some wood to the fireplace."

Jacob called, "Hey, Luke. Why don't you put the clean dishes away?"

"Got it," Luke answered.

Julie loved feeling like a needed part of this new family of hers. These brothers treated her like she belonged with them. Their acceptance warmed her heart. With everyone lending a hand, the kitchen was clean in just a few minutes.

James tucked his turkey into the roasting pan and slipped the pan into the oven.

Soon Emma was back at her elbow. "Now we have family time around the fireplace. Walk with me." She wrapped Julie's hand around her arm and led her to the sofa facing the fireplace. Emma sat on one end, placing Julie in the middle with Josiah on Julie's left. The other boys all found a place in a chair or on the floor.

Once everyone was settled, James spoke for Julie's benefit, "This is our time to share what we are thankful for from the last year. We take turns from oldest to youngest."

Julie asked, "Where do I fit in line?"

James chuckled, "I'm not sure. I know you're never supposed to ask a woman how old she is, but you're like my sister, right?"

Julie laughed with him, "I'm nineteen."

"I'm nineteen, too," interjected Tim.

Emma added thoughtfully, "Your birthday is July 25th, and Tim's is June 3rd. That makes him almost two months older."

"Luke turned eighteen in August, so that puts you between Tim and Luke," James declared. "Emma, we're all set whenever you're ready."

Emma took a deep breath, then began. "On the first Thanksgiving after we were married, Daniel started this tradition of gathering together around the fireplace to remember God's blessings. We have continued this tradition every year since. Even in the hardest years, we always found something to be thankful for. This year has been the hardest of all. Losing him broke my heart. I never would have made it without you boys. I knew you were grieving, too. For many of you, he was the only loving father you had ever had, and he was so proud to be your dad."

"This Thanksgiving, I want to remind you how thankful I am to be your Mom. God brought each of you here in different ways, but every one of you was meant to be part of our family. Thank you for stepping up and running the ranch when I was consumed with my sorrow. I have not forgotten how each one of you found me every day for a hug. You constantly reminded me that I was loved. Julie, your coming was a ray of sunshine. You may not be able to see, but you have a glow about you that spreads joy. Every one of you is an answer to prayer, and seeing you here just reminds me again that God is faithful. His ways are perfect. His sovereign hands guide every detail of our lives, and we can trust Him because He loves us. He never promises us that hard times won't come. Rather, He promises us that when those hard times do come, He will be with us every step of the way." She paused for a moment, "All right, James, it's your turn."

One by one, they each took their turn, telling stories about how they were thankful for one another as they recounted God's blessings. When Josiah had finished, James rose to check on his turkey. As he opened the oven door, the smell of roasting turkey filled the room.

Tim commented, "Mmm, that smells good. I'm getting hungry."

"You're always hungry," Jacob remarked dryly.

"I'm a growing boy," responded Tim.

Emma laughed, "I certainly hope not. I just finished letting out the hem on your pants again."

James added, "This big bird will take awhile longer to cook. I wouldn't start the fixings just yet."

He rejoined the group around the fireplace and enjoyed listening to the conversations around him. As he looked over at his Indian brother, he couldn't help but smile. Buck was gazing at Julie as she chatted with Josiah. James knew Buck had meant what he had said in his prayer that morning, and he hoped God would answer Buck's prayer.

About an hour later, James peeked at his bird again. "All right, you all can start cooking." His brothers came into the kitchen and busied themselves in their tasks.

Buck approached Julie as she stood, "Are you ready?"

"Yes."

"What are you ready for?" Emma wanted to know.

Julie replied with a smile, "Making mashed potatoes." Buck led her to the kitchen where he unsheathed his knife, washed it, and began peeling and cutting potatoes. Julie put the potato chunks into the pot, covered them with water, and added a pinch of salt. Buck found an empty spot on the stove. As they waited for the potatoes to boil, Julie listened to the hubbub around her. The sounds of family, with talking and teasing and laughter, met her ears. This is what she had missed all those years, and now she was determined to enjoy every minute.

While Julie was still lost in thought, Buck spoke, "The potatoes are ready. Come."

After he drained the liquid off, Julie mashed while Buck added the butter, cream, salt, and pepper.

Julie asked Buck, "Do they look evenly mashed?"

Buck stood behind her, held the pot handle with his left hand, and reached around Julie to wrap his hand around hers on the masher. "They look good. We just need to blend in the potatoes around the edges a bit more." He guided her hand to incorporate the potatoes around the circumference of the pot. "Luke, would you hand me a bowl, please. Thank you." He set the bowl down next to the pot. "Here's a serving spoon. I'll lift the pot if you'll scoop the potatoes into the bowl."

Julie felt the sides of the bowl so she knew exactly where it was, then she began scooping the potatoes. When she finished, she asked, "Did I miss very much?"

"No, you did well. If I scrape the sides of the pot, I might be able to get another spoonful or two."

He turned to his older brother, "James, the mashed potatoes are done."

The last few of the brothers finished their sides just as the turkey came out of the oven.

"Perfect timing, as usual," remarked James. "Let's get the table cleared and set."

Everyone worked together to finish the table, and soon they were all seated. This time, Buck pulled out Julie's chair for her and sat down next to her. As they joined hands, Buck held out his right hand for Jacob and gently wrapped his left around Julie's hand. James sat at the foot of the table and prayed, giving thanks for the Thanksgiving dinner and all those joined around the table.

As Buck served Julie's plate, she remarked in Kiowa, *"This is the first time you have sat next to me at dinner."*

Buck answered softly, *"That is because I have a much better view of your smile from across the table, but on this day of thanksgiving I wanted to be nearest the one I am most thankful for."*

Julie blushed and changed the subject, "Emma, this cranberry sauce is scrumptious. Somehow, the flavor seems familiar."

"It should. After all, this is the Peterson secret family recipe. Your dad taught me how to make this sauce when I was a little girl," Emma replied.

"Really? My dad used to make this cranberry sauce?"

"Oh, he cooked quite a bit before he married your mom. She was so good in the kitchen that he didn't need to cook any more," Emma explained.

Julie's eyes misted with unshed tears, and Emma asked gently, "Are you all right?"

Julie nodded, "I just wasn't expecting such a strong connection to home. Thanksgiving with Mom and Dad seems like a lifetime ago."

After dinner, they all pitched in to clean up the kitchen once more. James delegated, "Luke and Josiah, go hitch up the wagon. We'll be out in a few minutes."

Julie asked, "Where are they going, Buck?"

Buck corrected her, "Where are we going? You are coming, too."

"All right, where are we going?" laughed Julie.

"To choose our Christmas tree."

"Our Christmas tree? How fun!" Julie grinned. The excitement around her seemed contagious, for everyone began talking and laughing as they put on their winter layers.

Buck was delighted with her enthusiasm, but cautioned, "Dress warmly. Sometimes it takes us awhile to decide on the perfect tree."

When everyone was bundled against the cold, they exited the house and climbed into the wagon. Buck lifted Julie into the wagon bed, where she sat between Buck and James beneath a thick fur blanket. Luke and Emma were up in the wagon seat.

As Luke drove, Julie asked Buck, "Does the wagon sound different because of the snow?"

"Yes. Jacob and I exchanged the wheels for sleigh runners yesterday. Your ears are remarkable by the way."

Before the sleigh had exited the ranch, James had started everyone in singing Christmas carols. Luke took the road south, then turned and skirted the southernmost border of the ranch, where there was a small forest of fir trees. He slowed to a stop, and everyone jumped down. Buck exited the wagon and instructed Julie as he brought her hands to his shoulders, "Jump a bit higher than usual to clear the side of the wagon." She jumped and soon felt her feet crunching through the surface of the snow. The festive smell of the firs surrounded them as Buck led her among the trees.

"Are you warm enough?"

"Yes, I am fine, thank you. Tell me about the trees."

"There are spruces and firs of all shapes and sizes. We are looking for one about seven or eight feet tall with full branches."

"I found one," called Tim.

Emma decided that Tim's tree was too skinny, Jacob's tree was too wide, but James' tree was this year's perfect tree. James held the tree upright while Buck and Tim worked the saw back and forth until they had severed the trunk. After the boys worked to get the tree into the sleigh, they all piled in around it with Buck lifting Julie into the sleigh again.

Julie took a big whiff, "Mmm. Fir trees smell heavenly."

Tim piped up, "I usually think they smell Christmassy, but my nose is too frozen to smell anything right now."

Julie's face was cold, too, but sitting between James and Buck shielded her from the chilly wind. Snuggled under the thick blanket, she was almost warm. She couldn't help the smile that shone on her face, for she had been waiting many years to celebrate the holidays with family again. Today she had finally realized what Emma and the boys had known from the beginning: she belonged here as a member of this family. She was truly home.

James seemed to know what she was thinking. He wrapped his arm around her shoulder and whispered in her ear, "I'm glad you've come home."

"Thank you, James. Me, too."

Several minutes later, Luke pulled the sleigh up to the front of the house. Everyone disembarked the sleigh, and Emma climbed the steps to open the door for the boys carrying in the tree. James and Josiah fitted the trunk into a galvanized bucket that Daniel had redesigned as a tree stand, and they moved it over to the right of the fireplace where it filled the corner of the room.

James asked, "How's that?"

"Turn the tree a bit to the left," Emma instructed.

The boys adjusted the angle.

"That's perfect. Now it's time to decorate."

71

Jacob brought the trunk of glass balls Emma's family had sent her years ago. The big strong hands of the boys who wrangled cattle and hefted bales of hay were gently holding the glass ornaments as they carefully hung them on the tree. When the last of the ornaments had been hung, James handed the star to Emma. He walked over to the tree, knelt on one knee, and offered his hand to Emma.

"Thank you for remembering, James."

Buck leaned close to Julie's ear and whispered, "Daniel always presented the star to Emma and knelt for her to reach."

Emma smiled as she slipped off her shoes, took James' hand, and stepped on his offered leg to reach the top of the tree. She carefully and securely placed the star that reminded all of them of the birth of their Savior. The finished product was beautiful. They stood around the tree and admired their handiwork for a few minutes before James broke the spell, "All right, time for evening chores." Every one of the boys hugged Emma and Julie and wished them "Happy Thanksgiving" one more time before exiting the house for the barn.

When the front door shut behind the last brother, Julie turned to Emma and enveloped her in a warm hug, "This has been the best Thanksgiving Day ever."

"The only way it could have been better is if Daniel had been here to share it with us." A quiet tear escaped down Emma's cheek.

"Weren't the boys sweet to remember every one of Daniel's traditions, even the Christmas star? They love you so much."

"Yes, it warms my heart to see Daniel living on in each one of them. I am truly blessed. Knowing you and the boys love me is the only thing that gets me through some days." Emma sniffed and wiped her eyes with the corner of her apron. "I'm sorry for my sadness on such a happy day."

"Never apologize for loving and missing Daniel," Julie reassured Emma.

The next day brought more snow, so the boys filed into the house one at a time after morning chores and hung close to the fire throughout the day. Buck found Julie and asked in Kiowa, *"Why is Emma sad?"*

"Her heart is missing Daniel a lot today. Remind her how much you love her."

Buck walked over to James and spoke to him quietly before he approached Emma and put his arm around her shoulders. "Do you need help with anything?"

Emma reached up and laid her hand on his, "No, but thank you, Buck."

Buck nodded, then said, "All of us are missing Daniel more the last few days, and I know you feel that more than any of us. Know you are not alone in your sorrow."

Throughout the morning, the boys made sure Emma was never by herself. They kept the conversations light-hearted. Once the kitchen was clean, Julie made a cup of tea and sat in the empty chair by the fireplace. The tree that filled the corner of the living room reminded everyone that Christmas was coming, and Julie overheard each one of her family talking in low tones hinting about the Christmas gifts they were going to give.

Chapter 8
Christmas

Julie was struck with the realization that she had nothing to give. She had no money to buy gifts in town, and she could not see to make anything. Even though Emma would probably give her some of her scrap yarn if she asked, about the only thing she could crochet with even stitches without her sight was a scarf. She was sure they already had scarves. What would she do? She desperately wanted to give them each something special, something uniquely from her, but what? While she was pondering her dilemma, Emma sat in the chair next to her and asked, "What are you thinking about?"

Julie jumped.

Emma laughed, "You must really be lost in thought. You always hear me coming."

Julie shared her thoughts.

Emma responded, "Your being here is enough of a gift for us."

Julie's eyes misted, "You don't understand. I want to give something."

Realizing how important this was to Julie, Emma thought for a minute, "Hmm. You could help me make the boys' scarves, and we could put both of our names on the package."

"You are sweet to offer, but I want my gift to be uniquely mine. I just need to think of a creative idea. I hope you understand."

"Of course, I understand. You want an expression of your love to them, and a shared gift just isn't quite right."

Julie relaxed, "Yes, exactly." She prayed silently, "Lord, you know my heart's desire to give a Christmas gift that shows just how much I love this family of mine, but I am at a loss to know what to do. Please help me find the perfect gift."

Julie didn't have to wait long for her answer. On the Sunday morning after Thanksgiving, Pastor Kendrick announced that the Wilson family was going to give their piano to the church now that their children who played were grown. He continued to share what a blessing the piano would be to the church and how his daughter Emily had agreed to play for the hymns. Julie had to do everything in her power not to shout for joy. She would give the gift of music. Emily could help her keep it a secret. She needed a plan.

After the service ended, Julie waited in the aisle to catch Emily. As she heard the swish of Emily's skirt, she spoke, "Emily, may I talk to you for a minute?"

"Certainly."

"Are we alone?" Julie whispered.

"All right, I know when I'm not wanted," interjected James. "I'll just go talk to . . . Somebody."

Emily laughed, "Now we are alone."

Julie smiled, "I have an idea for my Christmas gift for my family, but I'm going to need your help to make it happen and keep it a surprise."

"I'd love to help you." Emily hugged Julie. "Tell me, what are you planning?"

"I learned to play the piano when I was little, and I often tried to play simple melodies on the piano in the chapel at the blind school on the weekends. I'm hoping to learn

'Silent Night' and play for them after church on Christmas Day. What do you think?"

"I think they will love it. How can I help?" Emily asked.

"I'm going to need time to practice without certain ears listening, and I'll need your help with some of the chords."

Emily offered, "Why don't you come over with James on Saturday morning? He usually needs to leave just before lunch. You can stay through the afternoon, and we can get you home before dinner."

"Perfect. Thank you."

Buck noticed the change in Julie. For that matter, everyone in the family noticed the change in Julie. She had been rather pensive the last few days, and now she was fairly jubilant. No one could account for the change, but James wondered if it had something to do with her conversation with Emily.

On Friday afternoon, Julie asked James, "May I ride with you to Emily's house tomorrow?"

Now his interest was thoroughly piqued, "Sure, but may I ask why?"

"I'm planning to visit with the younger kids in the morning and spend some time with Emily in the afternoon."

James informed her, "I will need to leave just before lunch."

"Yes, Emily told me. She said they'd be able to get me home before dinner."

"No need. I can send Buck over to get you. Just tell me when," James instructed.

"Would five o'clock be all right?" Julie inquired.

"He'll be there."

When Saturday morning arrived, both James and Buck were waiting by the buggy as Julie exited the house. Buck strode up the steps to meet her and walk with her. He lifted her into the buggy while James climbed in the other side. Buck smiled at Julie, "Have fun with Emily today."

"I will," she answered with confidence.

"I'll be there at five."

"Thank you, Buck."

He took a step back from the side of the buggy, and James set it in motion. They traveled in silence for a few minutes when Julie remarked with a grin, "You know, you drive almost as well as Buck."

James laughed, "I'll take that as a compliment." Then he added, "Listen, when we get there, you'll need to talk me through helping you down like Buck does."

"Of course. Thank you for thinking of me."

A few minutes later, they arrived at Emily's house. James hopped down and came around to Julie's side. She stood to face him. "Okay, what do I need to do?"

"Put my hands on your shoulders. Now put your hands around my waist. When you're ready, tell me to jump, and you can lift me over and down."

"Buck makes this look so easy. Okay, jump." He lifted her up and over and placed her feet on the ground.

"Thank you, James." James walked her to the front door. She heard the door open and the swish of a skirt come out. "Enjoy your time with Emily this morning." Julie walked into the house toward the sound of the kids.

James looked at Emily with a puzzled expression and asked, "What are you two up to?" Emily just smiled. Their morning visit was uninterrupted by Emily's younger siblings. As he prepared to leave, he told Emily, "I really enjoyed having you all to myself for a little while. Maybe I'll bring Julie every week." They laughed together, then James climbed into the buggy and waved good-bye. "See you tomorrow," he called as he moved the buggy back down the driveway.

Emily entered the house just as Julie was serving lunch. "This is a surprise. You didn't have to make lunch."

Julie smiled and nodded toward Emily's siblings, "They did most of it. I just supervised. They wanted to do something sweet to help you."

"Well, you were both sweet and helpful." Emily walked around and hugged each one of her siblings. She sat Julie down in the chair next to her and asked her brother to pray.

After lunch was eaten and the kitchen cleaned, Emily put the oldest of her sisters in charge and walked with Julie to the church. "The Wilsons just delivered the piano to the church yesterday afternoon, so I haven't had a chance to play it yet. I do hope it's in tune after the move."

"How long has it been since you've played?" Julie asked.

"The Wilson family encourages me to play each time we visit them. The last time was about three weeks ago. I'm thrilled that I'll be able to slip over here and practice more regularly. Playing the piano is one of my favorite pastimes." Emily added, "Julie, we're at the steps."

Julie bumped the bottom step with the toe of her shoe. "These steps I know. Seven steps up." She lifted the hem of her skirt a couple of inches and climbed the steps smoothly."

"You amaze me."

Julie laughed, "If you had seen me the first year I was blind, you wouldn't have been amazed. I tripped, ran into everything, spilled anything in my hands, and felt frustrated all the time. I had not realized just how independent I had become until I was forced to depend on everyone around me. The blind school taught me how to compensate for my lack of vision and learn to do some things on my own. God changed my heart, helping me to find joy despite my blindness."

They stepped into the church and walked to the front.

"Nevertheless, you are an encouragement to me, and I'm glad we're friends. How interesting to think that we both play the piano! Does any of your family know that you play?"

"I think Emma went to one or two of my recitals before she married Daniel and moved West, but they were so long ago that she might not even remember. None of the boys have any idea."

Emily helped her up the step to the platform and led her over to the piano. "Would you play for me first?"

The piano bench scraped the floor as Emily pulled it out to sit. Soon the beautiful strains of "Amazing Grace" filled the room. Emily played with smooth arpeggios and lovely phrasing. Now it was Julie's turn to be amazed.

When the last note faded, Emily rose, "Your turn."

"Don't be too disappointed," Julie requested. She sat and fingered the keys to find her place before playing the melody with her right hand. Then, she added the right-hand harmony. "Emily, what is the broken chord progression for the key of B-flat?" Emily shared the piano bench with Julie and talked her through the chords for her left hand. By the end of their practice time, they had created a simple but lovely arrangement of "Silent Night."

Emily smiled, "Your family will be so surprised. I can't wait to see their faces."

"You'll have to tell me about their reactions. I just hope we can keep it a secret until Christmas."

"James suspects something, but he won't get any hints from me. As long as we're over here together, my family will think I'm practicing."

"That reminds me. Buck is coming to pick me up at five o'clock. What time is it now?"

"Almost quarter-till. We should head back to the house in case he's early," Emily suggested. They walked back over to the parsonage just a few minutes before Buck arrived.

Julie gave Emily a hug. "Thank you."

"You're welcome." Emily whispered, "We'll have to get you over here another time to practice before Christmas."

"Yes, that would be a good idea," Julie agreed.

Buck walked up and asked, "Are you ready?"

"Yes, thank you."

As Buck reached for her hand, he again noticed her smile. James was right, she and Emily were definitely up to something.

He lifted her into the buggy and laid a thick fur blanket across her lap before climbing in the other side.

"Are you warm enough?"

"Yes, I'm comfortable, thank you," Julie replied.

"Did you enjoy your time with Emily?" Buck asked.

"I did. The kids and I played and made lunch while Emily was visiting with James. Apparently, the younger girls have a great time interrupting the two of them." Julie laughed, "I had my hands full distracting the kids enough to leave them alone for the morning. After lunch, Emily and I had a chance to visit for a while. I am blessed to have her for a friend."

Buck smiled, "James would agree with you."

"Thank you for coming to get me."

"You are welcome."

After Buck came to a stop in front of the ranch house, he climbed down and circled around to help Julie. James was right; Buck did make disembarking the buggy easy. Julie did not take him for granted. After her feet crunched through the soft snow to the ground, she lifted her face slightly and smiled, "Thank you."

"Anytime," Buck replied as he guided her up to the front door. "I'll unhitch the buggy and be back in a few minutes."

After dinner, the boys made their way to the barn for their evening chores. James walked up to Buck's side and asked, "Did Julie tell you what she and Emily are up to?"

"No."

"Emily wouldn't say anything either." James looked disappointed.

Buck admonished him, "Whatever their secret is, we should honor them enough to let them keep it."

"Yes, I suppose you're right, but that won't keep me from wondering what it is."

Emily orchestrated another practice time two weeks later on a Friday afternoon. By the end of their time together, Emily decided that Julie was more than ready for her performance. Christmas was only one week from Sunday. Though Emily and Julie were sure James and Buck suspected something, the men had asked no more questions. Julie was confident their secret was still a secret, and she couldn't wait for Christmas to come.

When the family gathered together after dinner on Christmas Eve, Emma announced that since Christmas fell on Sunday, they would wait until after church for the gift exchange. Christmas morning dawned with a light snow falling, and the snow was still falling as the family left for church. Buck arrived at the front door of the ranch house and greeted Julie, "Merry Christmas."

Julie smiled, "Merry Christmas to you, too."

James opted to drive the sleigh, so Buck lifted Julie into the back of the sleigh, and Buck and Jacob sat next to her. James tucked Emma under the blanket as she sat next to him on the wagon seat, and Buck and Jacob tucked Julie in with them under a shared fur blanket. As James set the sleigh in motion, Julie could hear the swish of the sleigh runners in the snow and a new sound - bells. James had added a few bells to the horses' harness. They were the perfect addition for Christmas Day.

As Buck helped Julie out of the sleigh and walked with her up the church steps, Julie was never so glad to be on his arm. The precipitation and cold temperatures had made the steps icy. She had just begun to feel her foot slip when Buck caught her around the waist. His movement was so quick and smooth that no one else even noticed what had happened. When they had entered the church, Buck helped her remove her winter coat. "Are you all right?" he asked quietly.

"Yes, thanks to you," Julie replied. "I'm so glad you were there with me."

"Me, too."

When Buck led Julie up the center aisle to their seat, Emily found her and quickly whispered in her ear, "I'll ask James to keep your family here after church."

"Oh, I hadn't thought of that. Thank you for remembering." Julie breathed a small sigh of relief as she slipped into the pew and sat next to Emma.

Julie was happy that Christmas Day fell on Sunday this year. Meeting for worship to celebrate Jesus' birth just seemed fitting. As Buck listened to her sing her beloved Christmas carols, he thought her voice was beautiful.

Pastor Kendrick preached about Jesus as the Perfect Lamb. He began by discussing the sacrificial lambs of the Old Testament and the story of Abraham and Isaac and the ram caught in the thicket, reminding everyone that only the blood of a spotless lamb could atone for sin. That atonement was limited and needed to be repeated regularly.

Jesus was born our Perfect Lamb. He was not born in a palace, but in a stable. He was not laid in a royal crib, but in a manger. The angels did not appear to the nobility, but to the shepherds. Why? Heaven knew that Jesus was born to die as a Lamb. God's Son came to live a sinless life that He might die once for all on the cross and permanently pay the penalty for our sin. To celebrate the gift of His birth was to celebrate Him as our Savior.

Julie was once again filled with awe that God Himself would come to earth to die for her. Her mind recreated the scene in the stable as a young mother held her newborn son and sang him a lullaby. This was the setting of the first "Silent Night."

Pastor closed the service by leading the congregation in "Joy to the World," and everyone rose to wish each other "Merry Christmas" before heading home to be with their families on this holiday. James walked across the aisle from where he was sitting with Emily to tell his family not to leave yet.

In a few minutes, Emily stepped up to Julie, "Your family and I are the only ones left. Are you ready?"

"My hands are shaking."

Emily reassured her, "You will do just fine. You played the arrangement perfectly last week."

"All right, will you walk with me?" asked Julie.

"Of course," Emily replied with a smile. She took Julie's hand and guided her to the platform. Emily motioned to their families to sit.

Tim leaned toward Jacob, "I wonder if she's going to sing." Jacob shrugged in response.

When the shuffling stopped, Julie spoke, "Christmas is a time of giving. Jesus gave everything He had for us, and I wanted to somehow give part of myself to you. I am so blessed to call each of you my family. My gift doesn't come with wrapping paper or ribbon, but I hope you will enjoy it." She turned to Emily, who led her to the piano. The scraping of the piano bench as Julie moved to sit echoed throughout the room. Once she was settled, Emily moved to sit beside James on the front pew.

The church was perfectly silent as Julie felt the keys to get her hands in the right position. She took a deep breath and began playing her arrangement of "Silent Night." Emily looked up at James, then over at the rest of Julie's family. They were awestruck. Buck was the most composed of the bunch, with his eyes glued to Julie and a smile growing on his face. Emily and her friend had succeeded in keeping their secret.

Julie played as if her song were the lullaby Mary had sung to Jesus. The notes were just as she had practiced, but the music spoke a deeper message. When her last note faded away, not a sound could be heard. As she rose from the piano bench, Tim started clapping, then everyone else joined him. Emily jumped up to meet her and give her in a quick hug before walking with her to her family.

Emma came up to her first. "Your gift was perfect. The music was beautiful. I had almost forgotten hearing you play when you were little."

"Emma, are you crying?" Julie asked gently.

"Yes, well, maybe a little. Tears of joy, you know." Emma hugged Julie.

One by one, her new brothers surrounded her, asking her questions about when she learned to play the piano and when she had found time to practice.

James stood next to Emily, "I knew the two of you were up to something, but I had no idea. Julie, your song was beautiful."

"Thank you, James. I'd never have been able to play without Emily's help. She's wonderful."

James looked down at Emily, "Yes, she is." Emily gave him a sweet smile.

Julie leaned toward Emily and whispered, "There are too many people moving for me to hear. Where is Buck?"

Emily laughed and whispered back, "He's standing right in front of you with a smile on his face."

Julie blushed.

As James escorted Emily to the back of the church, Buck finally spoke, "Julie, your gift was the best Christmas gift I have ever received. You never stop amazing me, for your courage allows you to accomplish the impossible."

There was the unmistakable sound of pride in his voice. He led her down the aisle to help her don her coat. Before they exited the church for the sleigh, he whispered, "Merry Christmas."

Julie smiled, for she knew Buck well enough to hear the words he didn't say, "Merry Christmas, Buck."

Chapter 9
Meeting Wind Dancing

Christmas turned into the new year, and soon winter descended in earnest. The boys still slept in the bunkhouse, but other than necessary chores, their waking hours were spent in the ranch house. Julie listened to her family discuss the plans for the springtime activities on the ranch. Since she had never been on the ranch during the busyness of spring, she peppered them with questions about everything from calving and branding to preparing and planting the garden.

When the first glimmers of spring finally arrived, so did the fervor around the ranch. James delegated well. Jacob and Josiah were in charge of preparing and planting the garden for Emma and Julie. Buck and Tim repaired the fences. James and Luke inspected the herd and began moving the expectant cows to their own pasture. Not only would they be able to give these cows hay with more nutrients, but having them isolated from the rest of the herd helped during calving, too. Once calving began, the boys worked in shifts around the clock, checking on the herd every two hours and quickly drying off and tagging the newborn calves soon after birth. Luke somehow managed on a couple hours of sleep a night as he was called upon frequently to help with the delivery and assessment of the new calves.

Once the calving was finished, branding began. Emma took Julie down to the south pasture fence and described the scene as Josiah and Luke manned the fire and branding irons while the other four roped the calves and held them for the branding of the Rugged Cross Ranch emblem. Several days later, the last calf was branded, and final plans were made for the annual cattle drive to Kansas City. Emma and Josiah made a trip to town for the supplies to stock the chuck wagon.

That afternoon, a man from town galloped his horse up to the barn. James heard the commotion and came out to meet him. Breathless, the man asked, "Is your Indian brother here?"

James turned to Tim, who had stepped up behind him, "Get Buck." To the man on horseback, he asked, "What is this about?"

"Sheriff Stewart has a riot on his hands. Something about a group of Sioux attacking some white men or the other way around. I'm not sure. The sheriff asked me to come get Buck to translate so he can figure out what happened."

James disappeared into the barn and returned with weapons and his saddled horse. When Tim and Buck rode up a few minutes later, James said, "Buck, there is trouble in town, and the sheriff needs you to translate. Tim, here's your Colt .45 and your rifle. You and I will ride with Buck. I want us to be armed in case Will needs help getting Buck out of there safely."

When they rode into town, the tension was already mounting. The arrival of another Indian didn't help. James was glad he and Tim were on either side of Buck. The sheriff summoned Buck into his office, and James and Tim stood guard out front.

Buck entered to find a band of Sioux braves in one jail cell and a group of seven white men in the other. The white men were jeering loudly, but Buck ignored them and spoke to the Sioux in their tongue. When he explained that the sheriff was a man of honor and truth, they agreed to answer the sheriff's questions. Will interrogated the Sioux braves with Buck's help and found that they were innocent of any wrongdoing. The white men in the next cell had attacked their hunting party for no reason.

When the sheriff released the Sioux, the leader of the outlaws shouted at Buck, "This isn't over. You will live to regret the day you helped those filthy Indians!"

Buck gave no response. He was not intimidated. This wasn't the first time he'd been threatened because of his bronze skin. He shook Sheriff Stewart's hand and exited the way he had come, again flanked on either side by his brothers until they were safely home.

James had asked Jacob to stay at the ranch to cover the daily chores and perimeter fence checks, while the other five packed to leave at dawn for Kansas City with the part of the herd headed for market. Emma and Julie cooked an early breakfast for everyone. As the other boys exited the house to mount their horses, Buck found Julie and spoke in the Kiowa tongue, *"I will keep your smile with me until my return."*

Julie understood his meaning, *"I will miss you, too. Be safe."*

Buck strode down the front steps and mounted Wind Dancing. Jacob and the ladies stood on the front porch to wave good-bye as the men rode out.

After having the boys at the house so much during the winter, and having constant activity during the early spring, the ranch now felt too quiet to Julie. The fact that she missed Buck didn't help. Jacob came to the house for his meals. He teased Emma and Julie that they kept him talking so much at mealtime he barely had a chance to eat. In truth, he was happy that the only time he needed to go to the lonely bunkhouse was to sleep. He even missed the cacophony of snores that usually met his ears at bedtime.

Emma and Julie kept themselves busy planting the garden and doing the spring cleaning. Two weeks later, when their entire "to-do" list was exhausted, the cattle drivers arrived home.

The next morning, Buck came by the front porch to resume his morning walks with Julie. When they stopped at their usual boundary, a good distance from the corral fence, Buck turned to Julie, "Do you ever miss your rides on Nutmeg?"

"Every day."

"If you wish to overcome your fear, I will help you."

"I'm not sure," Julie replied hesitantly.

"Do you trust me?"

"Yes."

Buck smiled, "Good. We will take this one step at a time. Literally. Let's take one step toward the fence."

They took one step together and stopped. "Are you okay?"

"My mind cannot understand how one step can make my heart race like it is, but yes, I am okay. You must think I'm foolish to be so afraid."

"On the contrary. To face a fear that has controlled you for many years takes great courage. I could never think you foolish."

Day by day, one walk at a time, one step at a time, Buck and Julie gradually inched closer to the corral fence.

Then one day, Buck said, "We will reach the fence today. Are you ready?"

Julie spoke honestly, "I think so."

Buck smiled, "You will be just fine. I have someone who wants to meet you."

As they approached the fence, Buck moved directly behind Julie, brought her hands to the fence rail, placed his hands next to hers, and stood quietly while she gathered herself.

Again he asked, whispering near her ear, "Are you ready?"

"With you, yes."

Buck's soft whistle yielded the sound of hoofbeats getting closer. Julie gripped the fence and took a deep breath.

Buck leaned close again, "I am right here. Nothing will hurt you. You are safe."

Julie jumped a bit when she felt the sudden warm breath of a horse blow on her hand, but she felt Buck behind her, sure and steady. She did feel safe, protected. She was ready. Buck seemed to sense what she did not say, gently lifted her trembling right hand from the fence rail and guided it in his strong hand to the warm, soft muzzle of the horse.

He spoke in the soft rhythm of the Kiowa tongue, *"Desert Rose, I'd like you to meet Wind Dancing."*

"Wind Dancing. A perfect Kiowa name. Hi, there."

The horse Julie could not see was an American Paint horse, standing sixteen hands tall, with color patches of dark brown and white. His mane and tail bore a bit of both colors. He was indeed beautiful. They stood there for many minutes, petting Wind Dancing, with the first of Julie's fear melting into trust again. Buck knew it would be many moons until her fear was gone, but the healing had begun, and he could not be more proud of his Desert Rose.

Chapter 10
The Kiowa Village

"Indian rider coming! Josiah, get Buck," called James. Josiah rode to the back pasture to bring Buck to the barnyard.

James met the Indian rider as he arrived and used the hand signs Buck had taught him to say, "Welcome. Running Buck comes." The visitor nodded and waited for the Buck to approach. Buck began the conversation in his native Kiowa.

"Hello, friend."

"Hello, Running Buck. Chief Running Bull sends his greetings and the message that his people camp near Buffalo Hill."

"Tell Chief many thanks for the message. Are other Kiowa villages camped nearby?"

"Chief Soaring Eagle and his people have camped in the plains near the river forest."

"Follow me. I have a gift for the Chief."

Buck rode with the Indian over to the smokehouse, dismounted, and brought out a large beef roast that he wrapped in canvas and tied to the Indian's saddle.

"Peace."

"Peace."

The Indian messenger rode away.

That afternoon, Buck spoke with James about the trade they had initiated last summer for another horse. They had been waiting for the nomadic Indian villages to make their trip south as they followed the buffalo herd migration.

Now they had arrived. Early the next morning, Buck donned his buckskin and rode out to his Kiowa village to meet with Chief Running Bull. The purpose of his meeting was twofold: to renew the peace agreement between them and to orchestrate the resolution of the trade of cattle for a horse. Not just any horse. Cinnamon. Nutmeg's filly. A horse carrying Wind Dancing's foal. His village was the one that received Cinnamon from a neighboring Kiowa village those years ago. He would never forget that horse. What a strange name for an Indian horse! There had been rumors that she was bewitched. When none of the other warriors had wanted her, he had been the one to train her. Cinnamon's temperament was just as Julie had described Nutmeg: smart, gentle, agile, and sure-footed. Now he knew the rest of the story.

When he had chosen Cinnamon last summer, the chief was almost relieved. That was about a month before he had ever even met Julie. Now as he considered God's leading in his life, even in the smallest details, he couldn't help but smile. Julie was slowly overcoming her fear, and Buck wanted her to have Cinnamon when she was ready to ride again. He brought Cinnamon home and temporarily renamed her "Red" so Julie wouldn't find out who was in the barn. He wanted to be sure she felt neither rushed nor intimidated. When she was ready, Cinnamon would be there.

After walking with Julie and taking her by to visit Wind Dancing, he left her to her work on the porch while he quietly circled the house to find Emma. "Emma, I need your help with something."

"Anything, Buck. What is it?"

"I want to do something special for Julie. I will be visiting her Kiowa village in a couple of days and wish to ask her Indian mother to make a pair of moccasins for her. I want my visit to be a secret, and the moccasins to be a surprise, but I need a tracing of her feet to take with me."

Emma smiled, "Don't worry. I'll take care of it. I love surprises!"

"Thank you, Emma."

Emma's thoughts were consumed with how to get a tracing of Julie's feet without her knowing. Julie nearly always wore her old moccasins in the house like slippers, saying how comfortable they were because they fit like a glove. She was blind, but her hearing was excellent, and she didn't miss much. Even now, Julie had probably changed into her moccasins after her walk with Buck. She was never barefoot, except . . . Yes, that might work!

Slipping in through the back door and into the kitchen, Emma found Julie wiping the table and preparing to set it for lunch. Emma walked over to the creaky drawer that held the paper and pencils and pulled out three pieces of paper and a pencil. The first piece would be her rouse. "Julie, I want to start a shopping list. Have you noticed anything we need?"

"Hmm. We're starting to get low on sugar and bread flour."

"Sugar and bread flour. Got it. Anything else?"

"I can't think of anything else right now, but I'll let you know if I do."

"Thanks, Julie. Do we have anything that has to be done this afternoon?"

"I had planned to sweep the front porch, but it can wait. Why?"

"I feel like taking a nice, warm bath."

"That does sound lovely."

"Then it is settled. Baths after lunch." Emma was pleased. *"So far, so good,"* she thought to herself.

Julie helped Emma draw her bath first. As Emma sank into the water, she sighed happily. Julie had been right; it was lovely. A warm bath was always soothing and relaxing. When Emma finished, she carefully and thoroughly dried the floor, then double-checked on her paper and pencil before getting more hot water to warm the bath again. Julie took her turn next. As Julie stepped out of the tub, she took two steps before drying off her feet. After Julie exited the bathroom, Emma quietly reached for the two pieces of paper, laid one on each footprint, and lifted them to reveal two perfect impressions. She had to act quickly now before they dried. "Oh, I need to add salt to the shopping list, too."

Emma walked over to the counter, scribbled salt on the list, and carefully traced the footprint patterns. Her plan had worked!

Emma met Buck in the barn later as he was bedding the horses for the night. "Here you go, Buck. Tracings of both feet."

A look of surprise turned into one of his easy smiles. "Thank you, Emma. You don't know what this means to me."

A few days later, just as dawn was coloring the horizon, Buck and Wind Dancing rode out for another visit to a Kiowa village, this time to the one ruled by Chief Soaring Eagle. His purpose was to find Julie's Kiowa parents. Julie had once mentioned that her mom made the most beautiful moccasins in the village. Buck carefully tucked the drawing of her feet in his saddlebag.

His heart beat a little stronger in his chest when he thought through his plan. The plan that even Emma did not fully know. A smile spread across his face as he rode closer to the village. Wind Dancing seemed to understand Buck's anticipation and increased his speed.

Buck reached the village by noon. He greeted the warriors and met with Chief Soaring Eagle. When he was dismissed, he asked a brave to take him to White Feather and Runs Like the Wind. When he met Julie's Kiowa family, he told them his story and respectfully asked permission to marry Desert Rose, explaining that it was the white man's custom to speak with the bride's parents first. When they gave their blessing, he handed Julie's foot tracings to White Feather and asked if he could buy a pair of handmade moccasins for Julie's gift. She was delighted.

Chapter 11
Helping Luke

The ranch hand brothers had taken a small part of the herd on a three-day drive to the neighboring Indian villages, leaving only Luke to oversee the animals while they were gone. Red, the newest addition to their stable, was close to delivering Wind Dancing's foal. Luke had asked to be the one to stay, knowing that the upcoming full moon might send her into labor. Before he headed to bed, he had checked on all the stable animals, but felt the need to check on Red one more time. She was pacing in her stall. He entered and placed an experienced hand on her belly. Yes, she was getting close. Tonight would be the night.

Luke returned to the bunkhouse for his pillow and blanket, planning to stay close to Red. After dropping them on the cot in the stable, he lit another lantern and hung it on the hook in Red's stall. Humming a soothing tune for Red's benefit, he examined her once more. She had a few hours yet. He should try to get some sleep.

Red's whinny woke him a couple of hours later. As Luke rose, he could hear that she was still pacing. After splashing some water in his face and washing his hands and arms, he took his post in Red's stall. Luke loved caring for the animals, even if it did mean losing sleep from time to time. Humming while he examined Red's progress, he knew the new foal would be making an appearance soon.

As Red dropped to the soft straw to complete her delivery, she became restless and snorted in pain.

"Easy, Girl."

Something was wrong.

"I'm just checking your baby, Red. Easy does it."

As Luke reached in with his gentle hand and long arm, another contraction contorted her womb. He could feel the foal's head, but the umbilical cord was twisted around its neck. He worked for a few minutes, but could not undo the tangled cord. The foal was moving, so it was still alive. Every minute was critical. He needed help.

"Easy, Girl. I'll be right back."

Luke came rushing into the dark house. "Emma!"

"What is it, Luke?"

"Red is having trouble. I need you now!"

"Could I be of help?" Julie inquired.

Luke knew of her fear of horses, but he also knew he needed the extra hands. "Come quickly." He left the house and ran back to the barn to the stall where life and death hung precariously in the balance. By the time Emma and Julie arrived, Luke's arm had disappeared past his elbow. He quickly explained, "The cord is wrapped around the foal's neck, but I can't feel it well enough to move it. Emma, can you try to calm down Red?"

As Emma made her way quickly to Red's head, Julie offered, "May I try to move the cord? Remember, I see with my hands."

Luke reached for her and gently pulled her down to where he was sitting on the straw.

"Here." He encompassed her hand with his and guided it to the offending cord. She quickly but gently felt the path of the cord and found the tangle. Julie began to loosen the cord.

"I've got it." She gently lifted the cord around the foal's head.

"Good girl." He was truly impressed. "Now, Red, let's deliver this baby."

Julie carefully moved around to Red's head and accepted the rag Emma pressed into her hands to clean her arm. Once Julie was settled, Emma was available to help Luke. He looked up briefly when he heard the most soothing lullaby and saw Red's head resting in Julie's lap while she rubbed the horse's muzzle. In his amazement, he couldn't help but smile.

"One more contraction, and you can meet your little one." A minute later, the mare delivered a healthy filly. "Red, you have a baby girl. Good job, Mama."

The three of them quietly slipped out of the stall and leaned their arms on the top of the stall door, leaving the new mare to clean and care for her filly. Within minutes, the filly was standing on wobbly legs and starting to nurse. They witnessed the miracle of new life. Luke softly described the scene for Julie.

A short while later, Emma announced, "I'm heading back to bed. Are you coming with me, Julie?"

"If it's all right, I'd like to stay awhile longer."

Julie looked relaxed enough, despite the fact that her fear of horses had kept her from the barn until now. Emma was still hesitant to leave her alone.

Luke noticed the concern on Emma's face, "I'm wide awake and up for the day at this point. I'll be here in the barn starting my morning chores, so I'll be close if Julie needs anything."

"All right, then. Good night, you two." Emma turned and departed the barn.

Julie spoke softly, not wanting to break the spell of the beauty she knew was in the stall before her. "Thank you, Luke."

"You're welcome. If you need anything, just ask."

Luke left her at the stall door and began his work.

When the rest of the crew arrived home later that morning, Luke told Buck how Julie had saved the filly's life and kept Red calm during the delivery. He teased his brother.

"Before last night, I was happy for you. Now I'll admit I'm a bit envious." Buck clapped Luke good-naturedly on the shoulder.

Buck found Julie still leaning against the door of Red's stall, as if she were looking at the mare and filly, and said in Kiowa, *"Today, Desert Rose has become the soaring eagle."*

Julie smiled, and rested her head on her folded arms, exhausted.

Julie told Buck that she felt a strange connection to this horse. She yawned, "Friendship born from adversity, I guess."

Within minutes, she dozed off. Buck carried her to the cot there in the barn, and Luke covered her with his blanket. Buck and Luke kept an eye on her while they tended the horses.

After waking from her nap in the barn, Julie asked, "Where am I?"

Luke leaned over a nearby stall door to reply. "You are on the cot in the barn. You fell asleep. Buck carried you here, and I tucked you in."

"So last night wasn't a dream?"

"If you mean your saving the filly's life, no, it wasn't a dream. And Buck and I could not be more proud of you." He exited the stall and paused as she stood, then came along beside her and wrapped her hand around his arm, "Here, let me to walk with you to the house."

"Thank you, Luke."

Buck looked up from where he was pitching hay to watch Luke escort Julie home. Her nightdress and robe were filthy from the delivery, and her hair was disheveled with bits of straw clinging to it. He knew she'd be mortified if she saw her reflection in a mirror, so for one brief moment, he was glad she was blind, for her sake. As far as he was concerned, her appearance was evidence of her great leap of courage last night. When her fear of horses was put to the test, the love she had for the mare and foal overshadowed her fear. Hadn't he read, "Perfect love casts out fear"? The time had come for her to learn the mare's true identity.

After Julie had a chance to freshen up a bit, she changed into a clean blue cotton dress. With her neatly brushed hair pulled back in a blue ribbon, Julie wandered her way back to the barn. She entered the barn doorway, but not knowing where to go, she simply stood there taking in all the sounds and smells around her. She was still standing there, framed in the doorway, when Buck approached with a load of fresh straw. He paused for a moment and smiled.

Finally, he entered the barn with the straw. "Good morning, Sleepyhead."

Julie smiled shyly.

"I've got the bedding for the new filly. Come with me."

Buck's arms were full, so Luke came along beside Julie to guide her. "I'll walk with you."

Luke escorted her to the closed stall door. "Thank you, Luke."

"You are welcome."

Julie could hear Buck spreading the straw bedding on the stall floor while he spoke to the mare and filly. He exited and softly closed the stall door again then eased Julie up to the door so they could both rest their arms on the door's top ledge.

"I have a secret to tell you."

"What is it?"

"You told me you felt a connection with this mare. You were right." He continued slowly, "This horse's name is not Red; it is Cinnamon."

He watched Julie's face as a look of astonishment appeared.

"Cinnamon? My Cinnamon?"

"Yes."

"How did you find her?"

"She was brought to my Kiowa village years ago, and I raised her and trained her with Wind Dancing."

"Chief Soaring Eagle sold her to your village." Julie spoke with awe. She paused, then added softly, "I often prayed that God would give her to someone with a gentle hand like mine. Now, years later, I learn He answered that prayer through you. God is amazing."

Buck nodded. "Yes, He is."

Cinnamon walked over and nuzzled Julie's hand to get petted while the filly nuzzled Cinnamon to nurse.

"Now she is yours again."

"She is mine?"

"She never truly belonged to anyone else. What will you name the filly?" Buck wanted to know.

"What does she look like?" Julie wondered.

"She is a solid chestnut like her mare."

"Who is her sire?"

"Wind Dancing."

Julie laughed, "I should have guessed. Well, since she looks more like her mare, her name should reflect that. What do you think of Cinnamon's Spice? We could simply call her Spice."

"Spice, it is."

"Buck, will you teach me how to ride again?"

Buck was silent. Julie could not see his smile.

"What is it? You will teach me, won't you?"

"You have come so far from the one who jumped at the sound of every whinny. Yes, I will teach you, but Cinnamon won't be ready to ride until Spice is older. You will need to ride Wind Dancing."

Julie smiled, "Do you think he'll mind?"

"Not at all. He'll love every minute. Some days, I think he likes you more than me. We'll start this afternoon."

Chapter 12
Learning to Ride

A couple of hours after lunch, Julie changed into a riding skirt and made her way to the corral fence, where she folded her arms on the top rail, rested her chin, and stood just listening to the sounds around her. This is where Buck found her.

"Wind Dancing is saddled and ready for you. I know that you often rode bareback before, but having a saddle will give you much more control."

"I trust you. Whatever you think is best."

Buck smiled down at her. He guided Julie over to the hitching post. Wind Dancing greeted her with a soft nuzzle.

"See, I told you he likes you better than me."

Julie laughed and rubbed the horse's soft nose, "You had better show Buck some love, too, or he's going to be jealous."

Just then, Jacob paused as he was passing by, walked up to Julie's other side, and spoke, "You do know that Buck never lets anyone else ride Wind Dancing or even touch his saddle. You must be pretty special."

Julie turned to Buck. "Is that true?"

"Yes. All of it."

Julie blushed and turned her attention back to Wind Dancing.

Buck smiled again and began his instruction. "Our goal today is to teach you how to mount and dismount safely. Run your left hand along Wind Dancing's neck until you reach the saddle. Good. Now follow the edge of the saddle down to the stirrup. Good. Bring your left foot up into the stirrup. Now follow the edge of the saddle toward his mane to find the saddle horn. A little bit higher. There. That's it. Now hold the horn, push up with your left leg, and swing your right leg over his back. Beautifully done. Are you okay?"

"Yes, I feel like I'm higher than I remember, but I'm okay."

"I didn't adjust the stirrups quite short enough. Let me readjust them for you."

He lifted her foot from the stirrup.

"Bend your knee for a moment."

She moved her leg out of the way. While Buck shortened the stirrup, Julie bent forward to pet Wind Dancing's mane with her right hand.

"There, how's that for length?"

Julie straightened her leg and found the stirrup again.

Nodding, Buck commented, "That looks better. Let me get the other side."

Julie lifted her foot out of the way as Buck came around. She took in all the sounds around her: the squeak of the leather, the jingle of the stirrup buckle, the metallic sound of Wind Dancing rearranging his bit, the swish of his tail to bat at a fly, and the hoofbeat as he moved his weight.

Buck finished his adjustment. "How's that?"

Julie replaced her right foot in the stirrup and stood up, lifting a couple of inches above the saddle seat. "Perfect." Buck hadn't needed to tell her what to do; she just instinctively remembered.

Buck had never seen anyone else on Wind Dancing, but Julie looked as if she belonged there. She was relaxed and smiling, talking to the horse and petting his neck, and, Buck noticed, already gripping him with her knees. He needed to teach her to dismount, but she looked so comfortable in the saddle that he ventured, "Would you be all right if I walked Wind Dancing around the barnyard?"

"Yes, I'd like that."

As Buck untied the reins, he spoke to Wind Dancing, "All right, big guy, slow and steady for the pretty lady."

He guided his horse slowly, walking backwards at first to be sure Julie was okay. Other than her hand gripping the saddle horn, she still looked completely relaxed. He continued to walk for a few more minutes then returned to the hitching rail. Wind Dancing had obeyed his every command, not even trying to speed up. The horse seemed to know the precious cargo he was carrying.

Buck talked Julie through the dismount, and her first lesson was complete.

Each afternoon, Buck walked Wind Dancing a little further and a little faster until he was confident Julie was ready to take the reins. She was still blind, however, and would need a pair of seeing eyes in the saddle with her. He planned a special ride for her on Saturday morning.

That day finally came. After Julie mounted Wind Dancing, Buck tied the reins together and hung them on the saddle horn.

He instructed, "Julie, lift your left foot."

When she did, he grasped the horn, slipped his left foot into the stirrup, and smoothly swung himself up into the saddle behind Julie.

"Today, you will learn to ride again. I am only here to guide you. The reins are on the horn. Remember to hold them in your right hand."

Julie might have been anxious at this milestone in her training, but she found she just couldn't be nervous with Buck behind her. She could not be in better hands than those of Buck and Wind Dancing. She picked up the reins and took a deep breath. Wind Dancing shook his head. He was ready to go.

Buck breathed in the hint of lavender from Julie's hair, "Whenever you are ready, turn him slightly left and give a little kick. We will head beyond the south pasture to a large grassy field."

"I'm glad you are here with me."

"Me, too," Buck added with a smile.

Wind Dancing shook his head again. Julie laughed at the horse's impatience. "All right, Buddy. Here we go." Julie made the kissing sound and kicked her heels. The horse followed her cue and began walking toward the south end of the ranch. Buck reached around a couple of times to steer him in the right direction, but Julie was doing well.

When they reached the field, Buck told her, "We have passed the south pasture. If you want to speed up, you may."

Julie kicked Wind Dancing into a faster walk for a few minutes then asked Buck, "Would it be all right if I went a little faster?"

Buck laughed, "This coming from the one afraid of horses. Yes, you can get him up to a canter, if you wish. I know Wind Dancing is ready."

Julie kicked him into a trot, then pressed with her left knee and kicked with her right heel. Wind Dancing responded with the smoothest canter. Julie was so happy that she laughed with joy. The smell of the grass and the feeling of the wind blowing through her hair brought back so many wonderful memories of her rides with Nutmeg. Her fear had completely vanished.

Buck sat behind her in wonder and admiration. Julie didn't need him to teach her anything; she handled Wind Dancing expertly. She must have truly been an amazing rider before her accident, and he was thankful that she had finally found her way back. When Julie had slowed Wind Dancing back to a walk, she exclaimed, "That was wonderful!"

"Yes, it was," he agreed. "Are you getting hungry for lunch? I brought a picnic."

"Did you? You are so thoughtful."

"Here, let me have the reins for a few minutes. There is a beautiful spot that would be perfect for our picnic, but the trail is a bit tricky."

Julie gave him the reins, and he leaned in to take control of his horse. She loved the feel of the wind in her face and the security of Buck against her back. This could not be a more perfect day.

About ten minutes later, Buck slowed Wind Dancing to a stop. He dismounted and tied the reins to a nearby tree while Julie dismounted. As Buck retrieved the picnic lunch from his saddlebag, Julie asked, "Where are we?"

"Ridge Hill. The smooth ascent on this side gives way to a cliff with the most beautiful view beyond. Do not take too many steps forward."

Julie stayed rooted where she was until Buck had spread a blanket for them and came back to walk with her.

Buck sat Indian-style, then looked over to see that Julie had done the same. He was momentarily surprised until he remembered that she would have naturally sat this way growing up in her village. One more reminder that, in many ways, she was Kiowa, too. The thought warmed his heart.

After Buck had distributed the food, he said, "Let's pray. Dear Lord, thank you for Your creation, for this food, and for the perfect friend to share it with. Amen."

As they ate, Julie requested, "Describe this place." She looked toward him with a teasing smile. "And use more than five words."

Laughing, Buck replied, "You know me well. We are sitting in the shade of a large oak tree on the crest of one of the highest hills in this part of the Oklahoma territory. About twenty feet to your right the cliff begins, and beyond that trees and plains stretch up to the horizon. Right now, everything is green, but in the autumn, the changing colors are spectacular from here."

Chapter 13
The Picnic Goes Awry

Julie was using her imagination to create the scene with brilliant yellows, oranges, and reds when her imaginings were interrupted by the sound of several sets of hoofbeats. Wind Dancing added his agitated noises to the mix.

"Buck, what's happening?"

"Seven riders are heading our way, and they look none too happy. Stand and get behind me."

Julie quickly moved behind Buck. He continued, "Uh, oh. They look like the men Will locked up a few months ago for trying to attack some Sioux braves in a hunting party. I was the one who translated the braves' testimony for Will, so they are probably targeting me. Wind Dancing is about thirty feet to the right of where we are standing. Get to him and go for help. He knows the way home."

"I'm not leaving you here. Come with me."

"Seven men would easily catch up with the two of us on horseback. That would put you in grave danger. Wind Dancing will fly with only you on his back. They want me. If you leave, they won't chase you. I cannot fight seven men and protect you. You must go. Now!"

The hoofbeats were getting closer. Julie ran toward Wind Dancing with her arms in front of her. When her hands touched the saddle, she followed the horse and the reins to where they were tied, pulled the slip knot free, and mounted Wind Dancing.

"Hey, look! The girl's getting away."

"Leave her. It's the Injun we want. That sorry excuse for a human being needs to be punished for testifyn' against us and for thinking he's actually good enough to be with a white girl."

"Wind Dancing, get me home. Fly!" The horse worked his way with quick, agile steps through the uneven terrain. As soon as the path flattened, he broke into a run. Julie bent down low over his neck and held on for dear life.

"Rider coming fast!" yelled Jacob.

"Only Wind Dancing can run like that, but that's not Buck. Something's wrong. Everybody get out here!" Tim called.

All of the brothers but Josiah were gathered to meet Wind Dancing's arrival and were all surprised to see that Julie was the one riding him. When he came to a stop, she was crying.

"Seven men are attacking Buck to punish him for testifying against them. He stayed back so I could escape. Please help him!"

"Where were you?" James needed to know.

"Ridge Hill."

"Mount up, boys! Let's go!"

In less than a minute, the boys headed out the way Julie had come, armed, and ready for a fight. They just prayed they weren't too late.

The intense emotions of the last several minutes caught up to Julie in a rush. She felt the blood drain from her face. She needed to dismount Wind Dancing.

Emma had heard the commotion and looked out the window just in time to see Julie faint and fall from Wind Dancing, landing on the back of her head. The horse stood perfectly still, with his sides still heaving from his run, as if he knew taking a step might hurt his beloved passenger. Emma ran to her and tried to wake her, but she remained unconscious.

Just then Josiah rode in from the other side of the ranch, where he had been inspecting the herd in the north pasture.

"What happened?"

"Thank goodness you're here! I'm not exactly sure what happened. Buck and Julie left for a morning ride, and only she came back. The rest of the boys rode out in a hurry. Just after they left, Julie fainted and landed hard. Would you please carry Julie up to her room?"

"Sure, Emma. Then I'll ride to town for Doc and the sheriff."

"Thank you, Josiah."

He gently lifted Julie and carried her upstairs. As the youngest of the family, he had a lot of big strong brothers to look up to. In this moment, as he carried the one Buck loved, he, too, felt big and strong, trusted with an important task. He laid her in her bed with Emma right behind him to tuck her in. Then he turned and exited quickly to make that ride into town.

James, Tim, Jacob, and Luke raced up to Ridge Hill. When they saw Buck, his shirt had been ripped off and lay in tatters on the ground, and his wrists were tied together over his head. The end of the rope was tied to a large branch of an oak tree. He was surrounded by the seven men, who were jeering at him and using him like a punching bag. The look on Buck's face was fierce, but he said not a word.

James initiated a plan. "Luke, circle around to their horses and take their rifles. Tim, as soon as Luke has the last rifle, untie the horses and send them running away. Then come and help us round up these ruffians. Jacob, come with me. Remember, we have the element of surprise on our side."

Jacob replied dryly, "Why do I not find that comforting?"

James and Jacob waited behind the bushes, ready to free Buck as soon as Tim caused the distraction with the horses. James whispered to himself, "Come on, Tim, hurry."

Jacob remarked, "Buck is strong, but even he can't handle much more of what they're dishing out."

"There go the horses. Hurry!"

Jacob ran straight to Buck and cut the rope holding his arms up. The rope seemed to be holding up his body as well, for as soon as the rope was cut, he doubled over in pain and crumpled to the ground. His first words proved that his thoughts were not for himself.

"Is Julie safe?"

"Yes, she came flying in on Wind Dancing and sent us to you."

"Stand there with your hands up, or we'll shoot!" yelled James.

The men, who had been distracted, realized they were surrounded and surrendered.

"Luke, get their guns." Without taking his eyes from the outlaws, he carefully collected their revolvers.

When they had tied each of the men's wrists behind their backs, the boys looked up to see Josiah and the sheriff riding in.

"Good work, fellas. Buck, are you all right?"

"I will be now that I know Julie is safe."

Josiah needed to update him, "Buck, Julie fainted and fell off Wind Dancing after our brothers rode out. She is still unconscious. Doc is with her." The look on Buck's face showed his concern.

Will instructed, "Buck, ride back with Josiah. Be sure Doc checks you out, too. The rest of the boys can help me get these thugs to jail."

Emma, who had been looking for the boys' return, spotted Josiah and Buck coming and sent Doc out to meet them.

Before Doc could say anything, Buck asked, "How is Julie?"

"We need to get you into the bunkhouse," was Doc's reply.

Josiah helped Buck dismount and grasped Buck's arm around his neck to help him walk to his bunk.

Realizing Buck wouldn't be able to climb up into his top bunk, Josiah said, "Here, lie down on my bunk." Buck groaned as his head hit the pillow.

Once more he asked Doc, "How is Julie? I won't let you examine me until you answer my question."

"You sure are stubborn. Julie fainted, fell from your horse's back, and landed hard on the back of her head. She is still unconscious but stable. We won't know anything more until she wakes up. Now, let me take a look at you."

Doc examined Buck closely. Other than a couple of cracked ribs and multiple bruises, he seemed to be all right. He would mend, but he was worried about Julie. The doctor wrapped his ribs and ordered him to stay off a horse for a few days. When Doc left the bunkhouse, Buck asked Josiah to help him with a clean shirt before he walked slowly to the ranch house. He could heal just as easily at Julie's bedside as in his bunk. He was determined not to leave her side until she woke. Emma understood. She made sure he was supplied with an extra pillow for his chair, water, and three meals a day. They went mostly untouched, but cooking kept her busy, for she was worried, too.

Two afternoons later, Will and James arrived at Emma's and made their way upstairs to where Buck was sitting. Buck looked up.

The sheriff spoke, "Buck, a Kiowa brave has been accused of cattle rustling. I think he's being falsely accused, but I don't know for sure because he doesn't speak any English. I put him in jail for his protection, but I need you to come translate for me so I can determine the truth about what happened."

"I do not wish to leave Julie."

James prompted, "What would she want you to do?"

Buck looked at Julie's sleeping face. He didn't even have to wonder what she would say. One of her favorite verses was Micah 6:8. "He has told you, O man, what is good; and what does the Lord require of you, but to do justice, and to love kindness, and to walk humbly with your God?" Seek justice. "I will go."

Emma appeared in the doorway. "I will not leave her until you return."

As Buck rose, Emma took his place at Julie's bedside.

About an hour after Buck left, Emma looked up in response to movement from the bed. Emma rose and smoothed Julie's hair back from her forehead. She spoke softly, "Julie, are you waking up?"

Julie scrunched her face, and her eyes fluttered open. At that moment, she let out such a gasp of surprise that even Emma jumped.

"What is wrong?"

Julie, still a bit groggy and disoriented, replied, "An excruciating headache, but Emma . . . I can SEE you!"

"Oh, my sweet girl, do you mean it! That is the most wonderful news! Not the headache, but you can really see?"

"You are wearing a dark blue dress."

Suddenly her thoughts sorted themselves. "Did the boys find Buck? Is he all right?"

Tears streamed down Emma's cheeks. "Yes and yes. He was roughed up quite a bit, but he is one tough young man. He has been here in this chair day and night until he was called away an hour ago to translate for a Kiowa brave that Will thought to be falsely accused. Don't move around too much. I'll send Luke for the doctor and be right back."

By the time Buck returned to the ranch, the doctor was just getting ready to mount his horse.

"I thought I asked you not to ride for a few days."

"Couldn't be helped. The sheriff needed me to translate. I took it easy. How is Julie?"

"A man with a one-track mind," Doc said with a smile. "She woke with a terrible headache while you were gone. You'll be delighted to know she is able to see again. How ironic that the same type of accident that stole her sight restored it. I have given her some pain medicine for the headache. She was sleeping again when I left her just now."

Buck gingerly climbed the steps back to Julie's room. Emma looked up from the chair with a smile. "Did you see Doc?"

"Yes. Can she really see again?"

"Yes. What is it, Buck? I thought you'd be thrilled."

"I am happy for her. My thoughts are completely selfish. I am concerned that she will be disappointed when she sees me with her eyes."

"Buck, you have nothing to worry about. You are a very handsome young man. Besides, Julie experienced a perspective few of us have. She learned to love the man you are on the inside first. That will make her love your handsome face even more."

Buck knew Emma was trying to encourage him, but he wasn't convinced. Still, he took his place at Julie's side and told Emma, "I will not leave her again until she wakes."

The thoughts of his heart continued to be bittersweet. Finally, he reached for the hand of the one he loved, gently lifting it from the sheet and surrounding it in his own.

He silently prayed, "Father, You know my heart and the love for this woman you have brought into my life. Her life was threatened because my skin is that of my Indian fathers. Please give me wisdom. If she refuses me when she sees my face, give me the strength to bear my broken heart, knowing it is a sign from You that I cannot adequately protect the one I love. If she were only to accept me, I would know great joy. Perform Your will in my life, I pray. In the name of my Lord Jesus, Amen."

He kept his head bowed another minute, then glanced up when he felt Julie stirring. She was smiling at him.

When their eyes met for the very first time, Julie spoke, "You are even more handsome than I imagined." The joy Buck had talked to the Lord about filled his heart and spilled onto his face as he smiled.

The next morning, their walks resumed. Buck laid Julie's hand on his offered arm as he had always done. Julie smiled. He still wanted her close at his side, though she no longer needed to be guided around the homestead. How different their walk was now that she could see! The colors were amazing! From the ranch house with blue wooden siding and white shutters and porch railing to the deep red barn with white trim, everything seemed new. Even the sun seemed brighter, and the sky seemed bluer than she remembered. Wind Dancing was waiting for them at the railing when they arrived. My, he was a handsome horse.

After spending a few minutes petting Wind Dancing, Buck and Julie strolled into the barn to see Cinnamon and Spice. When Julie first spotted Cinnamon, she marveled at how much she looked like Nutmeg.

Observing the look on her face, Buck asked, "What is it?"

"Cinnamon looks just like her mare, and Spice is beautiful, too. How much I have missed!"

A week later, when Doc finally cleared them both to ride again, Buck saddled Wind Dancing and tethered him to the hitching post in front of the ranch house. Julie put her mending down, rose, and walked to the porch railing.

Buck explained, "Instead of a walk this morning, I wondered if you'd like to ride with me."

Julie smiled, "I'll change into my riding skirt and be back in a minute."

When she returned, she descended the front steps toward Wind Dancing and looked up at Buck's smiling face. How she enjoyed actually being able to see his smile!

Buck gestured toward the saddle. "After you."

Julie mounted Wind Dancing and lifted her left foot so Buck could swing up behind her. Now that she could see, there was no reason for Buck to be there except that he wanted to be with her. That thought made her heart smile.

"Why don't we ride to the north pasture then gradually work our way around the perimeter of the ranch? You take the reins, and I'll just enjoy the ride," Buck suggested.

"Just point me in the right direction."

The day was crisp and clear with the smell of early fall in the air. As they rode together, Buck pointed out the various landmarks along the way. They started with the north pasture and traveled the outskirts of the ranch before

121

heading back to the corral. Neither of them was ready for the ride to end, but work never stopped on the ranch, and they both had responsibilities to fulfill.

After they dismounted, Buck turned to lengthen the stirrups for his long legs while Julie took just a moment to rub his horse's face.

"Buck, thank you for letting me ride Wind Dancing."

"You are welcome." He paused to look at Julie. "Jacob was right the other day. I've never let anyone else ride him."

"Why me?"

"I think you already know the answer to that question."

Julie blushed, and he finished adjusting the second stirrup.

Buck smoothly remounted. "I need to relieve Tim at the north pasture."

Julie gave Wind Dancing one last rub. "And I need to finish the mending."

"Maybe we could go for a walk after dinner?"

"I'd like that."

With a smile and a wave to Julie, Buck turned Wind Dancing back the way they had come. Julie paused just a moment, watching him gracefully ride away and returned to her basket of mending that she needed to finish before helping Emma with dinner.

After dinner, the boys rose and cleared their places at the table. Most of them then went into the living room to sit and relax. Jacob started a fire in the fireplace, because the early fall night was a bit chilly.

Julie turned to Emma, "Why don't you go in and join them tonight? I'll clean up."

"I'm not going to make you do all the work."

"You're not making me do anything. I'm offering. You've been working hard all day. Go and prop up your feet for a change. You deserve an evening off."

Emma smiled and reluctantly turned toward the living room. "It would feel good to sit."

Julie wiped down the table, poured some water into the sink, and added hot water from the kettle on the stove as she prepared to wash dishes. She heard movement next to her and glanced up to see Buck heading her way.

"You wash, and I'll dry," he offered.

"You worked hard today, too. Go sit and relax for a bit."

"Julie, you make it sound as if you loafed all day. I happen to know that you cleaned and reorganized the cellar before our ride this morning, after which you finished the entire basket of mending, filled and delivered a basket of food to the Johnson's, and cooked most of dinner. Besides, I have an ulterior motive. If I help you, you'll finish sooner, and we can have our walk."

Julie was about to debate some more, but she had no rebuttal. She relented and handed him the towel. They made fairly quick work of the dishes. She and Buck were a good team, after all. She wiped off the counters and emptied the dishwater into the bucket for watering the rose bushes before leaning over the chair where Emma was sitting to let her know she and Buck were going for a walk.

Buck was already at the front door, holding her sweater for her. She slipped into the long, cozy sleeves, and exited the door Buck had opened for her. The air was brisk, and the sky was clear and studded with thousands of stars. As soon as Buck put on his buckskin jacket, he reached for her hand.

Julie looked up at the man beside her. "You look lost in thought. Is something on your mind?"

"Do you think you've recovered enough for a half day's ride?"

"Yes, I think so. Why?"

"I recently learned that the village of Chief Soaring Eagle is camped about a half day's journey from here, and I wondered if you might like to take a ride with me to see White Feather and Runs Like the Wind."

The look on Julie's face gave her answer before she ever spoke a word. She was as excited as a little kid on Christmas morning. She turned to face him. When she spoke, the sentences came in rapid succession. "Do you really mean it? I would love to see them again! When can we go? I should wear my buckskin. This is going to be wonderful!"

Buck laughed, "I'm disappointed that you're not more excited."

Julie laughed with him.

"James said he could spare me on Friday and Saturday. I thought we could ride out on Friday morning. You could spend the night with them, and we could head back on Saturday after the noon meal."

"Where would you sleep?" Julie asked.

"I am perfectly content out under the stars."

"Are you sure you want to give up your days off for a long ride and a night's sleep on the ground?"

"If it means sharing time with you and giving you joy, my days off will be well-spent."

Julie smiled again, then suddenly realized, "Today is only Monday. I'd better stay busy this week, or Friday will never get here."

Chapter 14
Redeemed

The week seemed to creep by slowly, but Friday morning finally came. The boys were all in the barnyard and corral getting ready to begin their tasks for the day as Buck emerged from the bunkhouse dressed in buckskin and moccasins. Buck's clothing wasn't unusual when he was visiting one of the Indian villages, so his brothers barely noticed. He saddled Wind Dancing, tied on his bedroll, and packed some food in his saddlebag before he led his horse to the hitching post in front of the ranch house. One by one each of the brothers stopped their work in amazement. There, standing on the front porch, was Julie, dressed in a tasseled buckskin tunic with a matching split skirt and moccasins. Her hair was in two thick braids, with a thin beaded band and a small feather on each braid, and a beaded band that circled from her forehead to the back of her head. Other than her very fair skin, she looked every bit a Kiowa maiden.

Most of the boys had no idea of her years with the Kiowa, so they were rather stunned to see her dressed this way. James knew most of her story, for he had been the only one of the brothers living on the ranch when Daniel first brought her home, but he had never before seen her dressed in buckskin. Even Buck, who had grown up seeing Indian maidens in buckskin and had personally visited the village where Julie had lived, had never seen a maiden so beautiful as this. No wonder the chief's son had left a gift for her.

Julie descended the front steps as Desert Rose and greeted Wind Dancing first. While she rubbed his nose, she glanced at Buck and asked quietly in Kiowa, *"Why is everyone staring at me?"*

"They have never seen a Kiowa princess before."

"But I am not a Kiowa princess."

Buck smiled, *"You could have fooled me."*

He mounted Wind Dancing, and reached for her hand. "My stirrup is lower than you are used to. After you put your foot in the stirrup, push up a bit as you swing your leg over, and I will lift you the rest of the way."

She followed his instructions and soon found herself sitting right behind Buck in the saddle astride Wind Dancing.

"You may hold on to me, if you wish."

Julie circled one arm around Buck's waist and waved to Emma and the boys with the other.

She laughed and whispered to Buck, "I have the strange feeling I'll be a topic of conversation around the ranch today."

"I'm sure you're right."

Buck guided Wind Dancing through the ranch's front gate before he asked his horse for more speed.

Julie circled her other arm around him. "Are you all right back there?"

"Yes, I'm fine. It's a bit of a different perspective riding behind you. Are you sure you don't mind my holding on?"

"No, not at all."

Julie relaxed and enjoyed the ride. Buck handled Wind Dancing with deft precision. The horse responded even to his most subtle commands.

Just before noon, Buck guided Wind Dancing under the shade of some oak trees that bordered a stream. He spoke to Julie, "We will stop here for a few minutes. While we eat lunch, Wind Dancing can get some rest and water. Grab my forearm with both hands. Swing your leg over, and I will lower you down to the ground."

When Julie was safely on the ground, Buck dismounted and pulled their lunch from the saddlebag.

They sat Indian-style on the grass beneath the great oak branches. After Buck prayed, they ate together.

"We made good time this morning. We only have about another hour's ride ahead of us today." Then Buck added, "Have you ever ridden into the village with a man before?"

"Not conscious."

Julie was referring to her arrival after the wagon train massacre and after her accident with Nutmeg. She had been carried into the village unconscious both times.

Buck nodded, "Remember that riding behind me, you are entering the village under my protection. Only I am allowed to address the warriors as we ride in, even if you know them."

"Yes, I remember that custom now. Thank you for reminding me."

As Buck continued looking at Julie, a smile emerged.

"What are you thinking?" Julie wanted to know.

"You had confided in me the stories of your life with the Kiowa, and I have often been amazed how well you understand me as a result of your time in the village. I have always seen you as a prim and proper lady, well, except for the time you were up all night saving the filly."

They both laughed. "Oh, I must have been a sight."

"There have been times when I've had a glimmer of the true Kiowa in you, times when you would sit Indian-style as you are now, or speak to me in the tongue of the Kiowa, or talk of the customs of our people from your personal experience. Seeing you today, so comfortable in your buckskin and moccasins and braided hair, wearing beaded pieces that you yourself have made, I am finally able to see you with my eyes as the beautiful Kiowa maiden you are."

"How did you know I had hand-beaded these?"

"The art of a true artist will resemble the designer. I just knew."

As soon as they finished their lunch, Buck again mounted Wind Dancing and helped Julie up behind him. In an hour's ride, Desert Rose would see her Kiowa family, and she couldn't wait.

Desert Rose could see her village on the horizon. She pointed and spoke quietly in the tongue of the Kiowa.

"There is the home of my people. We are getting close."

"Remember that since you are not my wife, I will not have the liberty to interact with you as I usually do."

"I understand. You must keep your honor as a Kiowa warrior by respecting all of our customs. I promise not to be offended by your silent nods and stoic face."

As they approached the village, four warriors came out to meet them. One of them was Runs Like the Wind. Desert Rose was glad Running Buck had reminded her to stay silent, or she would have surely greeted her Kiowa father. Running Buck slowed Wind Dancing to a stop before the men and spoke, *"I am Running Buck. We come as friends and request permission to lodge with you tonight. Desert Rose wishes to visit with White Feather and Runs Like the Wind."*

One of the warriors asked, *"Is this your wife?"*

"No, but she does enter the village under my protection."

The warrior nodded, and Runs Like the Wind added, *"Her mother will know great joy today. You may enter our village."*

"Many thanks." Running Buck walked Wind Dancing slowly into the village of tepees and maneuvered him to the corral fence.

He offered Desert Rose his arm and instructed, *"Desert Rose, dismount as before."*

She landed softly and went over to give Wind Dancing a thank you hug while Running Buck dismounted. She glanced up at Running Buck, who seemed to read her thoughts. He nodded his permission for her to go, and she smiled and had to stifle a squeal of delight. She covered her mouth with her hand, turned, and fairly skipped to the closest cooking fire to ask the children directions to the tepee of White Feather and Runs Like the Wind. As Running Buck followed her with his gaze, he had to fight the smile that wanted to come. He turned his attention back to Wind Dancing, unsaddled and unbridled him, and released him among the other horses in the corral. He tossed his saddlebag over his shoulder and tucked his bedroll under his arm before he turned to follow Desert Rose at a distance.

Desert Rose approached the nearest fire and crouched down to be eye level with a young boy of about seven years. He was struggling to master a stick and ring game. *"That was one of my favorite games when I was your age."*

The boy looked up, saw her fair skin, and replied, *"You do not know how to play."*

"May I try?" Desert Rose asked.

He handed the pieces to her and was amazed to watch her get the ring spinning into the air and catch it again with the stick. *"How did you do that?"*

"The movement is in the quick spin and the flick of the wrist. Let me help you."

She squatted behind him and moved his hands in the right rhythm. The ring spun and flew, and he caught it with the stick. *"I did it!"*

"Yes, you did. Well done." Then she asked, *"Would you now do me a kindness and direct me to the tepee of White Feather and Runs Like the Wind."*

The boy pointed south. *"It is the fifth one over there."*

"Many thanks." She stood just in time to hear her name.

"Desert Rose, is that you?"

She turned to face her friend from long ago. *"Morning Song, seeing you brings me great joy!"* Desert Rose closed the gap between them and hugged Morning Song.

"Can you now see?" Morning Song asked in astonishment.

"Yes, the One True Great Spirit restored my sight just a few weeks ago."

"How are you here? Are you a wife?" she wondered.

"I have come to visit my family and my village. No, I am not yet a wife, but I have entered the village under the protection of Running Buck."

"Running Buck. That name sounds familiar. Have I met him?"

"I do not know. I did not meet him until I returned to the ranch of my white family. He grew up in the village of Chief Running Bull." After a pause, Desert Rose asked, *"Are you a wife?"*

Morning Song smiled, *"Yes, I am a wife of Gray Wolf, and I have two sons."*

"My heart feels much happiness for you." Desert Rose reached out and hugged her friend again. *"I have missed you."*

"I know you have missed White Feather also. She is in her tepee just down this way." She indicated the same direction the young boy had told her a few minutes before.

"Thank you. My heart has been aching to see her again."

"Go. We will talk again before you leave."

Because of her former blindness, Buck had not seen Julie interact much with children, and watching her gentleness with the little brave warmed his heart. As she reunited with Morning Song, Running Buck knew a moment of recognition. He would need to tell Desert Rose about it later.

Desert Rose walked south to the fifth tepee. She would recognize the painted pattern on the buffalo skin anywhere. She and her mother had painted this canvas together many years ago.

She stopped at the open flap and spoke, *"White Feather, it is Desert Rose. May I enter?"*

The sound of someone scrambling to her feet met her ears. Soon, a middle-aged Indian woman appeared through the flap. *"Desert Rose. My daughter. You have come home at last."* White Feather embraced her with tears of joy on her cheeks.

"Come. Visit with me."

Desert Rose followed White Feather into the tepee. *"May I help you with your work while we visit?"*

White Feather suddenly realized, *"You can see again!"*

Desert Rose laughed, *"Yes, my world was dark until just a few weeks ago, but the True Great Spirit has restored my sight."*

"Oh my daughter, my joy has just doubled. How have you come to the village?"

"Our ranch is about six hours ride to the east. One of Daniel and Emma's boys, Running Buck, learned where the village had settled and invited me to ride with him. I am here under his protection."

"How long can you stay?" White Feather wanted to know.

"Until tomorrow after the noon meal."

"The time sounds so short, but I will be thankful for what we do have. Does your father know you are here?"

"Yes, he was one of the warriors who met us as we arrived."

"Then he will be home soon to see you. Let us begin dinner so it will be ready for his return."

Desert Rose followed her Kiowa mother as she exited the tepee and walked to their cooking fire. Desert Rose turned to see that Running Buck had unrolled his bedroll on

131

the ground next to her parents' tepee. He was standing nearby with his arms folded. As his eyes met hers, he nodded his approval. She smiled and joined her mother at the fire, helping her start the stew and make the bread.

White Feather chatted with Desert Rose, as if they were together every day.

"I will save the important questions for later, when your father is with us. That will save you from answering them twice."

Desert Rose smiled at her mother's thoughtfulness and continued helping. When dinner was ready, they returned to the tepee just as Runs Like the Wind arrived.

As soon as he was inside the tepee, he strode to Desert Rose and hugged her.

"My arms have been aching to hold you since I first saw you approach the village. How we have missed you!"

"I have missed you both also."

"There are so many things I wish to know, but let us enjoy our dinner first. Before we go to the fire, I must tell you that Running Buck is a wise man."

"How so?"

"By having you come to the village under his protection, he is expected to know where you are at all times. That gives him permission to follow you around the village. Also, your being under his protection prevents anyone from leaving a gift for you without his consent."

"I have been back in the village only a few hours. No one would leave a gift for me."

"My daughter, you have always been pretty, but you have grown into a beautiful young maiden since you left. Running Buck knows that your heart is with your white family. If a warrior left you a gift, you would be forced to choose between leaving your white family forever or disgracing our family with your refusal. Running Buck's decision has eliminated this possibility. Within the last hour, I have overheard three different warriors planning their gift to you. Once I told them of Running Buck, those plans ceased. One of the warriors was

Gray Wolf. He confronted Running Buck, but even the chief's son received a refusal while keeping both your honor and ours still intact."

In surprise, Desert Rose replied, *"Even Gray Wolf? I had no idea."*

"You also have no idea how your kindness and beauty turn the eyes of everyone around you. I am proud of you, my daughter."

He turned his attention to his wife, *"White Feather, we must show our appreciation by inviting Running Buck to join us. I will soon return."*

He passed through the tepee flap and walked around the corner to where Running Buck was camped near the side of the tepee. *"Running Buck, you have shown our family great honor, and I invite you to sit at our fire for dinner."*

"Many thanks."

A few minutes later, Desert Rose and her mother exited the tepee with fresh bread and berries in two handmade baskets. Runs Like the Wind returned to Running Buck.

"Come."

Running Buck stood and followed him to the log near their fire. He sat next to Runs Like the Wind, and Desert Rose served the bread and berries while her mom ladled the stew. Running Buck looked up at Desert Rose as she served him, and he simply nodded his thanks.

When they had finished serving, Desert Rose and White Feather moved to the other side of Runs Like the Wind and waited patiently for the men to finish eating. After they completed their meal, the men stood and handed their empty bowls to White Feather and Desert Rose.

Runs Like the Wind turned to Running Buck, *"Come to the tepee. We will talk."* They walked slowly toward the tepee, allowing the women time to eat and giving the village warriors ample time to see the men talking together.

White Feather filled her bowl and sat next to Desert Rose, whose head was bowed in prayer.

When they began eating, White Feather spoke quietly, *"Running Buck says little, but his eyes speak much."*

"What do his eyes say?"

"That he cares for you."

After another bite, she added, *"Let us eat quickly, so we can enjoy family time."*

Desert Rose nodded with a smile. They soon finished and cleaned their bowls for the morrow before heading back to the tepee. The men were still talking in front of the tepee when the women entered, followed by Runs Like the Wind and Running Buck. White Feather and Desert Rose sat on the edge of the bed and picked up some beadwork weaving while the men sat cross-legged on the ground.

Desert Rose's Kiowa father turned to Running Buck, *"Here within this buffalo skin you may relax and speak freely. I consider the man who protects my daughter to be family."*

"Many thanks." Though his answer was still short, a weight visibly lifted from Running Buck's shoulders.

Runs Like the Wind addressed his daughter, *"Now tell me what has happened in your life since you left our home."*

Desert Rose began her story with the difficult transition back to the world of the white men, her time at the blind school, and the return to the ranch. She concluded by sharing how she learned to ride again and how her sight was restored. Throughout the story, her parents noticed Running Buck's name was mentioned many times.

When she finished, Running Buck added, *"Desert Rose has neglected to tell you of her great courage. When her fear of horses had kept her from even the front door of the barn, she pushed her fear aside to rescue the life of a filly during her birth."*

Desert Rose continued, *"Our God is so amazing! Do you know who the filly's mare is? My Cinnamon."*

White Feather interjected, *"Cinnamon? How?"*

"Do you remember when I would pray that Cinnamon would be given to someone who trained horses with a gentle hand? You had said the Great Spirit was too big to think about a horse and her trainer."

"Yes, I remember."

"God answered my prayer. Cinnamon was sold to the village of Running Bull and given to Running Buck to train. He has such a gentle hand with the horses, Mother, much like mine. Seeing him on Wind Dancing would remind you of me and Nutmeg. Then, a month or so before I came home to the ranch, Running Buck made a trade to purchase Cinnamon and have her carry his horse's foal on the prairie."

"By the time he returned to complete the trade early this summer, he knew the story of the day I became blind. He renamed Cinnamon so I would not know she was in the barn. Overcoming my fear happened with great patience, and he did not want me to feel rushed. Only after I helped deliver her filly did Running Buck tell me her name. That was the day I asked him to teach me to ride again."

Runs Like the Wind commented, *"But you could not ride Cinnamon so soon after giving birth."*

"No. Running Buck taught me to ride Wind Dancing, his horse that no one but he had ever ridden."

She looked over at Buck and saw his smile. Had it really been only a few hours since she had seen him smile? She had missed it.

Runs Like the Wind noticed Running Buck's expression also, *"There is the smile that has been carefully hidden today. I am glad it can return for a short while."*

Running Buck continued the story. *"Wind Dancing likes her better than me."*

They all laughed.

"In truth, I did not need to teach Desert Rose to ride. Once she was comfortable on Wind Dancing, she instinctively remembered what to do. She rides him with as much skill as I, and she is the only one I

would trust to hold his reins." Desert Rose's Kiowa parents did not miss the pride in his voice as he spoke of their daughter.

White Feather asked, *"How did you ride blind?"*

"Running Buck rode behind me to direct me and steer as necessary."

While he listened to her story, her father was pondering how Desert Rose could have such joy when her life had been riddled with such hardships. Runs Like the Wind asked what he wanted to know, *"What gives you your smile?"*

"Yes, I have been wondering the same thing," added White Feather.

Desert Rose thoughtfully replied, *"Remembering that the Lord is faithful and He loves me. With each passing trial, I felt that a little piece of me died: when my parents died, when I lost my sight, when Nutmeg died, when I left you, my Kiowa family, when I left Emma and Daniel for the East, when I left the students at the Blind School. By the time I was on the stagecoach to the ranch, not much of me was left. I was discouraged but knew I needed to go home. Then, somewhere in Missouri, while reading my Bible, I read David's words, 'Why are you cast down, O my soul? Hope in God.' That was the answer! My hope was not in my circumstances or my family. It was in God alone. Later, I was reading in Isaiah 43, 'Fear not, for I have redeemed you. I have called you by name. You are mine.' People around me have called me many names, some of them hurtful, but the only name that really matters is the one God himself gave me: Redeemed. When I know that I belong to God, I can trust Him with my life. That trust brings peace and joy."*

Runs Like the Wind remembered, *"This is the time of day you would read to us from your Bible. I have missed your words. What happened to your Bible?"*

Desert Rose replied, *"Morning Song borrowed it before the day I lost my sight. After that day, I forgot to ask for it."*

"Does she still have it?" her mother asked.

"I do not know. She had mentioned once about lending it to a friend."

Running Buck entered the conversation, *"I discovered the answer to your question today. Desert Rose, do you remember when you asked me how I came to know the One True Great Spirit?"*

"Yes."

"I told you then that I had been searching for the Truth when I visited another Kiowa village, met a maiden who spoke English with me and gave me a Bible. Reading that Bible led my heart to believe in the True God and accept His gift of salvation."

Still a bit confused, Desert Rose replied, *"Yes, I remember."*

He spoke slowly. *"Desert Rose, this is the village I visited. Morning Song is the maiden I met. You are the one who taught her English."* He pulled a book from his saddlebag. *"And the Bible she gave me was yours."*

Desert Rose looked at him in disbelief, for in his hand was the Bible the brave had found in the wreckage of her wagon train. God had used her Bible to bring her Running Buck to Himself. She breathed softly as her eyes filled with tears of joy, *"My God is wonderful!"*

The hearts of Runs Like the Wind and his wife had been gradually opening to the Truth of the Great Spirit for many years. He spoke, *"If the Great Spirit of which you speak gives Desert Rose such joy in the midst of her trials and cares about the very details of your life, even the training of a horse and the journey of a book, we want to know Him, too. Running Buck, would you teach us about your God and His gift?"*

Running Buck looked into the eyes of Desert Rose as he replied, *"Gladly."* He opened their Bible to John 3:16, read it in English, then translated and explained it in his native tongue. That evening, two more souls joined God's family.

A little while later, as the sun hung low in the sky, Running Buck spoke, *"For your honor and mine, I must excuse myself. The warriors need to see me camped outside your tepee before sunset."*

Runs Like the Wind looked up through the opening in the tepee, *"Yes, the time has flown like the eagle tonight."*

He stood, and Running Buck rose to his feet. They clasped wrists as the elder spoke, *"Many thanks, my son. Sleep well."*

Running Buck nodded with a smile, then corrected his facial expression before exiting the tepee.

Desert Rose and her Kiowa parents stayed up late into the night talking. Her heart was happy when she finally lay down in her former bed. She thought of the man who was sleeping on the ground just outside her tepee and knew she could not be more blessed than to have Buck as a friend and protector. He loved the Lord; he loved the Kiowa people; he loved his family at the ranch; and she knew in her heart that he loved her, too. Why else would he give up his days off for her and do the myriad of thoughtful kindnesses he was always showing her? Now that God had restored her sight, she now felt free to open her heart to love him in return. Though she realized love for Buck had already begun growing in her heart, she had no more need to feel guilty about her selfishness. If God's plan for her life included marrying Buck, she could now become the wife she should be. With a smile still playing on her lips, she fell into a peaceful sleep.

Morning came early, but Desert Rose was too happy to be tired. She had but a few hours left before they needed to leave, and she wanted to make the most of that time. She slipped from the tepee to prepare breakfast for her family. When she peeked around the side of the tepee, she saw Buck was sitting, reading their Bible, looking as if he had just woken up. The village was still and quiet, so Desert Rose chose to communicate with Indian sign. She used hand motions to tell him she was heading to the fire. He nodded, and she turned to go.

By the time White Feather and Runs Like the Wind were up, Desert Rose had prepared eggs, bacon, and porridge. She ducked into the tepee to let them know breakfast was ready. Her father wrapped her in a hug and said, *"You are going to make someone a wonderful wife."* He looked over and winked at his wife.

Laughing, Desert Rose replied, *"Many thanks, Father. Now come and eat before the food is cold."*

Runs Like the Wind exited the tepee and brought Running Buck to the family fire. Just like the night before, Desert Rose and her mother served the men and ate when they had finished. While the women washed the dishes and utensils, Morning Song approached Desert Rose. *"My dearest friend, my heart knows great joy to see you so happy."*

"Many thanks, Morning Song. Will you have any time to spare this morning? We will need to begin the trip back home after the noon meal."

White Feather interjected, *"Why not bring your boys by the tepee after breakfast? We can visit together."* Morning Song nodded her thanks.

Desert Rose and White Feather worked together to craft a beaded necklace in a white, blue, and raspberry pink pattern. Morning Song soon entered holding one little boy by the hand and wearing a newborn on a papoose board. Desert Rose laid down her work and knelt in front of the small boy.

"Morning Song, he is beautiful."

The proud mother smiled, *"His name is White Fox, and Coyote is sleeping on my back."*

"You are so blessed."

Desert Rose invited, *"Come and sit. I have an amazing story to tell you."*

Morning Song sat, and White Fox clung to her, looking at Desert Rose with his big brown eyes. *"Do not worry, little one, I am a friend."*

The little boy wasn't convinced.

Desert Rose smiled and began, *"Do you remember when you borrowed my English Bible for a friend shortly before the accident that sent me into a world of darkness?"*

"Yes."

"That Kiowa brave from a neighboring village was not only searching for English words. He was searching for the Truth. As he studied the words in the book, he learned of a Creator who loved him and offered forgiveness. That Bible led him to faith in Christ. He chose to pursue life with a ranching family in the white man's world, having heard about the owner's reputation as a Christian. There he continued to grow in his faith."

"How do you know all of this?"

"Because that brave was none other than Running Buck, the ranch belongs to my white family, and last night as we pieced the story together, he pulled my Bible from his saddlebag."

"I knew his name sounded familiar. What a wonderful story!"

White Feather added, *"The story does not end there. Running Buck taught us the ways of the True Great Spirit, and Runs Like the Wind and I accepted his gift of salvation. We three are now sisters in Christ."*

"Oh, White Feather, how wonderful!" Morning Song jumped up, startling White Fox, and hugged White Feather.

The three women continued to visit until time to prepare the noon meal. White Fox did eventually come to Desert Rose and sat in her lap, playing with her hands that were so fair compared to his own. They reluctantly left the tepee, and Morning Song gave Desert Rose one last parting hug. Both of them shed tears for a moment, but they had tasks to do and finally parted.

White Feather spoke to Desert Rose, *"Go ahead to the fire and begin preparations. I will meet you shortly."*

She found Runs Like the Wind. *"My husband, please invite Running Buck into the tepee so I may give him the gift without curious eyes seeing what they should not."*

He nodded and approached Running Buck. After he spoke quietly to him, Running Buck followed him into the tepee. There White Feather was waiting. *"Come and see,"* she invited.

Running Buck stepped over to where she was and saw the most intricately beaded moccasins he had ever seen.

He smiled, *"They are perfect."*

White Feather's eyes sparkled as she carefully wrapped the moccasins in a leather cloth and handed the package to Running Buck. She picked up the beaded necklace she and Desert Rose had just finished and handed it to Running Buck also.

"Please give this to Desert Rose on the day of your wedding as a gift from us."

He slipped it carefully into the folds of the package he held.

"Keep loving my daughter the way you already do, and you both will know great joy."

Runs Like the Wind added, *"Desert Rose is our most cherished treasure. We would not entrust her to just anyone. You are a man of honor in many ways, and we are thankful you have chosen her."*

"Many thanks. You both loved her unconditionally, and she is proud of her Kiowa heritage. If she accepts me, I will continue your unconditional love." Running Buck reassured him.

Her father spoke again as he placed a hand on Running Buck's shoulder, *"Do not fear, my son. Desert Rose will not refuse you."*

Wiping a tear of joy from her cheek, White Feather said, *"I must help my daughter with the meal, or she will wonder where I am."*

She exited the tepee, followed by Runs Like the Wind and Running Buck, who walked to his spot next to the tepee, slid the precious package into his saddlebag, and rolled his bedroll for the journey home. He gathered his things and made his way to the corral. His soft whistle brought Wind Dancing. Once his horse was saddled and loaded with the saddlebag and bedroll, Running Buck tethered him to the corral fence and returned to the family fire.

The noon meal was over too quickly. Desert Rose entered the tepee with her parents one last time for hugs, well wishes, and words of love before they strolled to the corral together as a family. Running Buck mounted Wind Dancing and helped Desert Rose mount behind him. Waving good-bye, Running Buck led Wind Dancing toward the entrance of the village, where he stopped for a moment to say *"Many thanks"* to the warriors on sentry duty.

Soon the village was behind them. When her quiet tears had stopped, Julie whispered, still in the Kiowa tongue, *"Desert Rose thanks Running Buck for her time in the village."*

Buck smiled the smile he no longer had to hide and replied in English, "You are most welcome."

When Buck stopped for dinner, they were just over an hour from home. Julie already missed her family and her best friend, but she was still happy to call the ranch home. Buck pulled their meal from the saddlebag, careful to keep his package completely hidden while he worked. They sat cross-legged in a grassy area near the bank of a stream to eat.

Buck prayed in Kiowa, *"My Lord and Creator, my heart is too full for English words. Thank You that Desert Rose experienced the joy of reuniting with her friends and family. Thank You that I was there to protect her and see her joy. Thank You that You used us to bring White Feather and Runs Like the Wind to You. Thank You for teaching us once again that Your sovereign hand weaves its way throughout every part of our lives. Thank You for our food. In the name of our Lord Jesus, Amen."*

Julie chorused her "Amen."

When their eyes met, Buck smiled, and Julie added her prayer of gratitude.

"Thank You, Lord, for allowing me to be able to see the smile that warms my heart."

While they talked about their time in the village, Buck reflected, "The hardest thing for me was to watch your joy and not be allowed to smile."

"Yes, I didn't realize how much I missed your smile until our reunion in the tepee. Runs Like the Wind told me you prevented the gifts of three warriors."

"There were more than three," he responded dryly.

"Really?" Julie was surprised.

Buck smiled at her reaction, "Gray Wolf was the seventh. Fortunately, after I refused the chief's son, the other warriors realized I wasn't planning to give my consent to anyone."

"Seven? I had no idea. Thank you for being there for me."

"You have no idea how beautiful you are. When you smile, your entire face glows, and your kindness and grace are evident in everything you do. Within hours of our arrival, you had turned every warrior's head in the village. I am glad you chose to ride with me."

Julie blushed.

"I couldn't ride with anyone else. Wind Dancing likes me." The horse whinnied, and they both laughed. They finished their dinner and remounted Wind Dancing for the final leg home. When they arrived at the ranch, Emma and the boys came out to meet them.

Buck unsaddled Wind Dancing. While he patted his horse's neck, Buck assured him, "You get the day off tomorrow. It is my turn to drive the buckboard to church."

He carried his saddlebag into the bunkhouse. Before he laid his saddlebag on the foot of his bed, he removed the leather-bound package and carefully placed it in his dresser drawer. The day of his gift would be soon. Preparations were nearly ready. He exited the bunkhouse and joined his family.

Emma invited everyone into the house for pie. The brothers peppered Julie with questions while Buck just sat and listened. His heart swelled with pride listening to Julie recount their time in the village and patiently answer her brothers' questions. He was glad he no longer had to hide the smile that kept appearing on his face. Buck's brothers now understood why he was so drawn to Julie, for they had not realized how much the two of them had in common. Emma sat in her chair by the fire and gazed at her family while thinking of Daniel and how proud he would be of all of them.

Chapter 15
The Gift

Just as the first light of the sunrise crept over the horizon five days later, Buck donned his moccasins, quietly collected the leather-bound parcel from his drawer, and walked silently to the front door of Emma's house. He carefully unwrapped the small bundle, removed the pair of handmade deerskin, fur-lined moccasins, and placed them on the doorstep. Inside one shoe he slipped a note: *"Running Buck leaves gift for Desert Rose."* When Buck returned to the bunkhouse to exchange his moccasins for his boots, only Luke was up.

"Is everything okay?" he asked sleepily.

"Yes," Buck replied with a smile, and he exited to get Wind Dancing ready for his morning ride to the south pasture.

After breakfast, Julie came outside to read her Bible. She spotted the gift, read the note, and wept tears of joy, hugging the moccasins to her. Emma came out of the house close behind Julie and found her still hugging the moccasins.

"I don't think I've ever seen anyone react so strongly to a pair of shoes."

"Oh, Emma. They're more than a pair of shoes. When a Kiowa warrior chooses a maiden to be his wife, he will leave her a gift. Don't you see, Buck just asked me to marry him!"

Emma threw happy arms around Julie.

"Julie, I am so happy for you. I must say, it's about time. No wonder you reacted as you did!"

Julie hugged her soft moccasins to her cheek once more then slipped them on her feet. A perfect fit.

She smiled as she sat in her familiar chair on the front porch and picked up her Bible. Her heart was full and happy. She opened to Genesis and reread the story of the marriage of Isaac and Rebekah. What a sweet love story displaying God's sovereign hand!

She thought about her and Buck's own story. Theirs, too, was woven by God's hand.

Suddenly, a new thought occurred to her. Buck had proposed according to Kiowa custom. Was he also expecting her to answer him by the same tradition? She knew the custom well. The betrothal gift was left for the maiden in the morning. If she accepted, she would wear the gift and prepare herself throughout the day, then enter the warrior's tepee at sunset. From that time, they were husband and wife.

But Buck lived in the bunkhouse. Surely he didn't want her to come to him there. Maybe his proposal was simply an homage to their common heritage. They did live in the white man's world, after all, and would need their marriage recognized legally. Now her smile had transformed into a puzzled expression as she struggled to know how to accept him. What should she do?

Buck wouldn't be by for a morning walk. He had told her yesterday that he was planning to leave at dawn to repair the back fence of the south pasture before lunch. She couldn't go to him there, not today of all days. No, today needed to be perfect, just in case.

Hmm. If she made lunch for the boys, she'd be in the bunkhouse serving, so he'd still be coming to her. Yes, that would work.

"Emma, would it be all right if I made Indian stew and biscuits for the boys' lunch?"

"Sure."

Julie smiled as she studied her beautiful moccasins for a few moments before heading over to the bunkhouse.

A couple of hours later, as she sprinkled the last of the herbs and seasonings into the stew, the boys began coming in for lunch. Julie was busy serving her brothers when Buck entered the bunkhouse. She looked up just in time to see Buck's gaze go immediately to her moccasin-covered feet and his face light up in a smile. When his eyes met hers, she couldn't help but smile in return. It was contagious.

Julie set the bowl of Indian stew in front of Buck and asked softly, "May I ask you a question after lunch?"

"Certainly." The aroma and flavor of the stew reminded him of his Kiowa village. "Mmm. This is good."

"What is it that makes this Indian stew?" Tim wondered.

Buck and Julie answered together, "Bear tallow." They met each other's gaze and laughed. There were chuckles all around.

When Buck had finished his lunch, he came over to Julie. "I only have a few minutes before I need to go check the herd. Would you take a short walk with me to the corral? Wind Dancing missed you this morning."

He cradled her hand in the crook of his arm, the way they had walked together when she was still blind, and they moved slowly toward the corral. "What is it that you wish to ask?"

"My moccasins are beautiful, and my wish is to accept them and the one who gave them."

Buck smiled.

"If we were in the Kiowa village, I would know how to respond, but we are here, and I am unsure what to do."

Thoughtfully nodding, he replied, "Let me ask you two questions. First, do you desire to be married in buckskin or a white dress?"

"Because I grew up Kiowa, I have no dreams of a wedding in a white dress. I would want you to wear buckskin, so I will do the same."

Nodding again, he continued, "My second question: Do you want to become one according to Kiowa tradition or would you rather wait for the ceremony of the white man?"

Julie blushed. "Is there any way we could combine the two? I do not want to wait to come to you, but I think it wise to be legally married according to the customs of white men."

Buck nodded. "Yes, I agree. Would you come to me tonight?"

"To the bunkhouse?"

"Trust me. Would you come?"

"Yes."

Buck's smile broadened. "Prepare yourself and meet me on your front porch at five o'clock."

"I will be there."

Buck mounted Wind Dancing and waved as he went to check the herd, and Julie went back into the bunkhouse to quickly clean up the table and dishes before heading over to the ranch house.

"Emma, will you help me draw a bath and wash my hair?"

"Right now?"

"Yes, I haven't much time. I'm getting married at five o'clock."

"Five o'clock? Today?"

Julie laughed at Emma's dismay. "Yes, today. That is the Kiowa way. One will wed on the day their gift is given."

"Oh, my! I suddenly have so much to do."

Still laughing, Julie asked, "Would you help me first?"

"Yes, of course. I still can't believe you're getting married today!" A sudden thought occurred to her. "What will you wear?"

"My best buckskin. But I want my hair in soft curls pulled back with a ribbon."

"Let's get to work."

A few minutes before five o'clock, Julie stepped out onto the front porch. Emma came out behind her. Julie noticed Pastor Kendrick's horse tied to the hitching post and spotted him in front of the bunkhouse speaking with Buck, who was dressed in his buckskin. Her brothers filed out of the bunkhouse one at a time all dressed in their Sunday best. James had evidently been to town to pick up Emily, who was waiting on the porch swing. She rose, walked over to Julie, and hugged her gently.

"I'm so happy for you, Julie."

"Thank you, Emily. I'm so glad you could be here."

Julie looked up to see Pastor and Buck heading their way. Julie's heart started to race with anticipation. How long had she waited for this day to marry the one she loved? They both climbed the steps to where Julie was standing. Buck opened a leather cloth in his hand to reveal a beaded necklace. Julie recognized it immediately.

Buck spoke quietly, "White Feather wanted you to have this on our wedding day." Julie lifted her hair, and he fastened it behind her neck.

"The delicate design on my moccasins is also the handwork of my Kiowa mother. When did you get them?" Julie wondered.

"During our trip to your village, she presented them to me when you went to begin preparations for the noon meal."

"But this design would have taken her several weeks. How did she know to make them?"

"Do you remember my visits to the Indian villages this summer?"

Julie nodded.

"The first was to my village to bring home Cinnamon. The second was to your village to meet your Kiowa family. Runs Like the Wind gave me his blessing to marry you, and White Feather agreed to make your moccasins for my gift."

Julie spoke quietly, "My world was still dark then, yet you would have married me though I was blind?"

Buck smiled, "Yes. The feelings of my heart have not changed because you regained your sight."

"I would have been unable to be the wife you needed."

"You would have been exactly the wife I needed. Whatever challenges your blindness would have created, we would have overcome them together."

Somehow, the overwhelming love Julie felt for her soon-to-be husband grew a bit more. Buck loved her unconditionally. She was so blessed.

Buck reached for Julie's hand and led her down two steps below where Pastor was still standing. As they faced one another, Buck held both of Julie's hands in his. The others gathered at the foot of the stairs, and Pastor began speaking.

"We are gathered here today in the presence of God and these witnesses to join these two in holy matrimony. You may say your vows."

Buck looked into Julie's smiling soft brown eyes a moment before he spoke.

"I, Running Buck Matthews, offer my gift to you, Julie Suzanne Desert Rose Peterson, and promise to love you and you alone as my wife. I will provide for you, protect you, and lead you in the ways of the One True Great Spirit as the Chief of our family. With you, I wish to be one before God until such time as the bonds of death separate us."

Julie was enraptured by the words he had spoken. At that moment, there was no one else in the world but Buck and the warm brown eyes that were looking into her soul. She continued.

"I, Julie Suzanne Desert Rose Peterson, accept the gift from you, Running Buck Matthews, and promise with all my heart to love you as my husband, to obey you as the Chief of our family, and to honor and respect you as my Kiowa warrior. With you, I wish to be one before God until such time as the bonds of death separate us. I wish to be completely yours and yours alone."

Emma quietly wiped a tear from the corner of her eyes and whispered to Emily, "Those words were beautiful."

Emily nodded.

Pastor continued, "You may now exchange rings."

From his pocket, Buck pulled out two circles of gold. He extended his hand so Julie could take his ring. Then he slipped Julie's ring onto her finger, saying, "For my Wife, my Love."

Julie slid Buck's ring onto his finger, saying, "For my Husband, my Warrior."

"With the authority vested in me as a minister of the Gospel in the territory of Oklahoma, I pronounce you husband and wife. Buck, you may kiss your bride."

Gazing intently into Julie's eyes, Buck replied, "Our first kiss will be ours and ours alone."

With a smile and an understanding nod, Pastor Kendrick concluded the short ceremony. "May I be the first to introduce to you Mr. and Mrs. Buck Matthews."

They descended the last two steps and were swallowed in congratulatory hugs and well-wishes. Several minutes later, Buck found Julie's hand and pulled her aside.

"The sun will be setting soon. Come."

He led her across to the corral fence, where Wind Dancing was tethered, bridled, and saddled. Buck mounted and extended his hand to pull Julie up behind him. She circled her arms around Buck. Everyone waved as they rode out of sight.

Julie asked softly into Buck's back, "Where are we going?"

"You will see."

Buck guided Wind Dancing down toward the river, where a new trail had been forged. They followed the trail through a wooded area and around a bend. Julie's breath caught in wonder and surprise, for there in front of them was a Kiowa tepee, complete with fire pit and hitching rail, with a small corral beyond.

"When did you build this?"

"I felled the trees and stripped the tepee poles several weeks ago and have been here working in the late afternoons. What do you think?"

"It's perfect."

Buck smiled at her approval as they dismounted, then added, "You watch for the sunset while I unsaddle Wind Dancing and build a fire."

The sunset started quietly, then one by one, the wispy clouds burst with color, until the entire sky was aglow.

"Buck, the sky is painted."

Buck stood up from where he was tending the fire and looked up in awe.

"God Himself added His brush strokes to the sky for us tonight. It is time. Come to me."

He moved closer to the tepee as Julie took the dozen steps to stand before him. In the glow of the firelight, she looked like an angel in buckskin. How could God have blessed him so much?

Julie looked up into the face of the man she loved with all her heart and spoke softly in the Kiowa tongue, *"Desert Rose accepts the gift from Running Buck."*

As he reached for her hands, he realized, "You are trembling. Oh, my Love, do not be afraid."

He enveloped her in his strong arms, holding her close against his chest and resting his cheek on her head.

Here in Buck's arms she felt protected and loved. She listened to the strong, steady beat of his heart until her fear melted away.

When Julie's trembling had ceased, Buck slowly released her. She looked lovingly into his eyes.

Buck spoke softly, "I love you. I have loved you since the day we first met. My heart has been aching to tell you, but I had resolved long ago that only my wife would hear those words from my lips."

Julie smiled, "Though you have not spoken the words, I have heard them often in your acts of kindness toward me, and I have seen them in your smile."

Buck smiled as he repeated again, "I love you, my Wife."

He gently lifted her chin and bent his head until their lips met. Their first kiss was indeed theirs and theirs alone.

Before the Painter's brush strokes faded from the sky, Buck led Julie into the tepee that would be their first home as husband and wife.

Chapter 16
The Attack

When spring came, so did the time for the annual cattle drive to the railhead in Kansas City. The air was still chilly, especially in the mornings, but starting in early spring ensured they would be able to ford the streams and rivers along the way before they began swelling with the melted snow. Luke was chosen to stay at the ranch to cover the necessary chores and care for the animals. James was the trail boss, leading the way. Josiah drove the chuck wagon with their food and supplies. The other boys took turns either flanking the herd as an outrider or eating the herd's dust as a drag rider. This year, they were moving five hundred head of cattle. James knew if their herd grew much bigger next year, he would need to hire some extra hands for the drive.

The weather was kind, allowing them to arrive on schedule, and the market prices were good. God was indeed blessing their ranch. After camping one night just outside of town, they began their trip home.

Julie was now expecting their first baby, their very own papoose, and Buck could not have been more proud. They were planning to tell the rest of the family at the picnic planned the Saturday after their return from the drive. Per Buck's request, Julie had been staying at the ranch house with Emma while they were gone.

One warm spring day, just before the men's return, Julie took a walk to the tepee, wanting to freshen things up a bit before Buck came home. While she was outside hanging the rug and blanket to air out, five rough-looking men on horseback rode up and startled her by asking gruffly, "Where's the Indian?"

Mentally kicking herself for being caught off-guard, she wasn't sure how best to answer.

"I asked you, where's the Indian?"

Not wanting them to know she was alone or exactly where Buck was, she replied simply, "He's not here right now. May I give him a message for you?"

That was apparently the wrong thing to say, for the leader of this malicious group sneered, "Yeah, we'll leave him a message."

Before Julie knew what was happening, she was nearly surrounded by these scoundrels who had quickly dismounted and approached her. Panicked, she took off toward the river trail in a dead sprint, or at least as much of a sprint as she could muster with the added pounds she was carrying around her middle.

She was hoping she could use this short cut to the ranch house and call for help before they caught her. It was not meant to be. Julie's foot caught on a root, and she tripped just as one of the men lassoed her like a calf. The way her skirt caught under her knee showed the round swelling of the growing baby.

The sinister scowl of the leader turned to raw hatred as he exclaimed, "Look! She's carrying his child. There are too many Indians already. Let's teach him a lesson he'll never forget."

Trapped like an animal, Julie couldn't get away, but that didn't keep her from fighting with everything she had. Through sobs, she tried desperately to protect her womb, but they wouldn't stop hitting and kicking her. Finally, she mercifully lost consciousness.

When she came to, the men were gone. Julie knew she had to get to the ranch house somehow, but she could barely move. Sharp stabbing pains ripped through her belly. As she looked up, she could just see the house in the distance through the trees.

"God, give me the strength to get to Emma."

Julie crawled to a nearby tree and used the strong trunk to help her stand. Step by painful step, she gradually moved closer to her goal. Finally, she summoned every ounce of strength she had left and yelled for Emma, who was hanging laundry on the clothesline.

Emma turned just in time to see Julie collapse to her knees and ran to her, hearing her sobs long before she could reach her.

"Luke!" Emma yelled.

Luke quickly approached the doorway of the barn and saw Emma rushing to Julie. He raced toward Julie, his long legs making up the distance between them. As he neared her, he could see the bruising on her face and arms, and he watched her brace her lower abdomen with her hand. Something was terribly wrong. The sound of her cries brought a noticeable tightness to his chest. What had happened?

A panting Emma reached Julie just before Luke arrived. She knelt beside her and gently placed her arm around Julie's shoulder. As Luke skidded to a stop next to her, Julie looked into Emma's face and spoke through her tears.

"Five men came looking for Buck. When he wasn't there, they surrounded me. I tried to get away, but I tripped, and they attacked . . ." Julie's words dissolved into more sobs.

Emma turned her tear-filled eyes to Luke, who was visibly wrestling with his emotions. All at once, he was overcome with a sudden rush of compassion, sorrow, and anger.

Emma addressed her son, "We need to get Julie upstairs." Luke nodded.

"Julie, I am going to lift you as carefully as I can." Luke wrapped one arm around Julie's back and the other under her knees and gently raised her in his arms and began walking smoothly with Emma alongside him. Julie still had one hand on her abdomen.

A few steps toward the house, Julie's entire body flinched as she cried out in pain. Luke stopped and looked down with concern into Julie's face. She met his gaze and answered the question he did not ask.

"The baby." Julie stifled another sob to continue, "Luke, I think I'm losing my baby."

Luke glanced over at Emma with anguish in his eyes, and Emma's eyes welled with sudden tears. Neither one of them had known she was expecting a baby. He resumed his steps with urgency. Emma moved ahead to open the door for Luke, then sped up the stairs to pull back the quilt. Luke laid Julie gently on her bed. As he slipped his arms from beneath her, a deep red color caught his immediate attention. He turned away from Julie so she could not see his arm and sleeve that had been stained with her blood. Emma gasped.

Luke assured her, "I will be back with Doc as soon as I can." He took one more look at Julie's bruised face and rushed out the door.

Luke mounted his horse and sped for town. After Emma tucked Julie in under the quilt, she began collecting the supplies she thought Doc would need if the baby did come.

When Luke arrived with Doc, he waited a moment and quietly followed him up the stairs. Luke rested his back against the wall in the hallway, where he was unseen by any in Julie's room. He leaned his head back as he closed his eyes and listened. The doctor had arrived just in time to deliver her stillborn baby girl, only a few inches long. He wrapped the tiny baby in a small bit of cloth and laid her on Julie's chest.

Luke heard Doc tell Julie that she had delivered a girl, and he continued to listen as Doc quietly explained the severity of Julie's injuries to Emma. When Doc finished, Luke slipped undetected from his clandestine hiding spot and walked over to the empty bunkhouse. He removed his bloodstained shirt and washed his arm, trying to keep his emotions under control. Since he was now alone, Luke finally let his quiet tears fall. He put on a clean shirt, then reached over to pick up his soiled one as he made his way over to sit on the edge of his bottom bunk.

As he turned the shirt in his hands, the folds fell open to reveal the blood stains on his sleeve. His heavy heart began to pray, "My Father, my heart aches for Julie. I cannot imagine what it is to lose a baby or to be beaten so severely. Please heal her injured heart as well as her injured body."

He took a deep, steadying breath, then continued, "Lord, thank you that I was there for her today, but she needs Buck right now. Please help my brothers to make good time on the trail so they might arrive home today, for Julie's sake. Be with my Kiowa brother when he hears the news. Comfort his heart. Buck is strong in many ways, but even his heart can break. Guard his actions. Do not let him choose vengeance. Show Yourself strong through him. In the name of my Savior, Amen."

As Luke finished his prayer, he could just barely hear the sound of distant hoofbeats.

"They're home. Thank you, Lord."

He dropped the stained shirt into the laundry basket and made his way to the barn to meet his brothers when they arrived.

As the men returned from the cattle drive, Tim noticed the doctor's horse tethered in front of the ranch house.

"Julie," breathed Buck, as he pushed Wind Dancing into a run for the house.

Tim called, "Don't worry, Buck, it's probably just a social call."

James looked at Tim with a concerned expression, "You shouldn't underestimate his intuition, especially when it comes to Julie."

Buck dismounted from his horse and ran full-speed for the front door, where Emma met him.

"Where's Julie?" Buck asked, starting to push past Emma. She grabbed his upper arms, not letting him pass.

"Buck, she was attacked by five men near the tepee this morning. They roughed her up quite a bit."

Emma sighed, with tears welling up in her eyes.

"Buck, look at me."

He moved his gaze from the top of the staircase to the woman standing before him.

"Julie lost the baby about an hour ago." The look of concern on Buck's face turned to utter agony. Agony for the wife he was not there to protect, agony for the little life they would now never know. Buck swallowed hard, trying to control his emotions.

"She is in the room at the top of the stairs. Doc is with her."

When Doc heard Buck climb the stairs, he rose and met Buck in the hall. Sudden tears filled Buck's eyes as he first spied Julie covered in bruises.

Doc spoke soberly, "Buck, I need you to hear what I'm saying to you. Julie suffered a lot of trauma today. She has lost a lot of blood. I don't know how she made it to the house."

Buck took his eyes from Julie to meet the gaze of the doctor. He was trying to understand, "What are you saying, Doc?"

"She miscarried your baby. And she may never be able to carry another baby again. Time will tell, but I need you to understand the severity of her injuries."

Nodding, Buck replied, "I need to see my wife."

With tears coursing down his cheeks, Buck strode into the bedroom and knelt at Julie's bedside. He wanted nothing more than to hold her in his arms, but he was afraid to hurt her.

"Oh, my Love."

Then he noticed the little bit of pink cloth Julie was holding gently to her chest.

"Is that . . .?"

Buck's words caught in his throat.

Julie tipped up her tear-stained face, "Buck, this is our little girl."

With a soft sob, she asked, "How can I love someone so much, when I will never know her this side of heaven?"

"You have known her. You carried her life. She has a part of you with her."

"And you."

The floodgate of tears opened. Buck leaned close to touch foreheads with Julie, and they cried together.

James climbed the stairs to find Emma leaning against the bedroom doorjamb, weeping softly as she gazed at Buck and Julie. "Doc told us what happened. I sent Tim for the sheriff."

"Thank you, James."

James looked up and saw Julie's face, almost unrecognizable beneath the bruising. Suddenly he was filled with a rush of pain and anger. "I can't even imagine what I would be feeling if that were Emily."

Emma admonished him, "James, don't let Buck be alone. Beneath his gentle exterior he is still a Kiowa warrior. Do not let him do anything he will regret."

"I will do my best."

When Julie finally succumbed to sleep, Buck rose and walked to the barn workshop. There he began building a small wooden box. James met him there and placed his hand on Buck's shoulder. Buck briefly looked up, then returned to his work.

"Is that for your little girl?"

Buck nodded.

"No words are the right ones. I am sorry."

Buck looked up again and saw tears in James' eyes. He nodded again, then with a voice made raspy with emotion, he requested, "Please send for Will."

"Already done. Tim should be back with him soon."

"Good. I will bury my . . ." His voice caught again. "my daughter. Then we will ride."

Knowing Buck was still at work fashioning the tiny coffin for his little girl, James exited the barn and began to delegate, "Luke, stay with Buck. Keep your distance when he goes to the Hill, but don't let him out of your sight. Jacob, make sure Emma has a loaded rifle at the house, just in case. Josiah, help me get fresh horses ready to ride."

When Buck finished his perfect little box, he walked to the house, paused on the front porch, took a deep breath, then entered. Upstairs, he gently lifted the tiny baby wrapped in pink from Julie's chest, raised her to his lips for one final kiss, and laid her ever so gently in the newly-crafted box.

He bent down an inch from Julie's sleeping face and whispered, "The men who did this will not go unpunished. Your Kiowa warrior goes to war. I will see justice done. I love you."

Buck gently kissed Julie on her forehead and removed the small box he had set on the dresser. He walked straight to the Hill, where Daniel was already buried. There he dug a second grave, barely able to see through his tears. Buck laid his daughter to rest, and covered the grave with soft earth.

Buck knew Luke had followed him, but Luke respected this time alone and stayed at the foot of the Hill, where he was partly obscured by the trees. He was glad Luke had come, even if just to remind him not to go rushing off by himself in vengeance. Now was his time to pour his heart out to the Lord. Buck yelled, a cry of anguish and pain, as he knelt at the new grave.

"God, why? Why did my Love have to suffer? Why did my daughter have to die? Why couldn't I have been there to protect her? Lord, I want to turn my back on You, but I cannot. My faith will not let me. Exercise Your justice. Let me listen to wisdom. Heal my wife, body and soul. Heal my broken heart. Help me to be still and know You are God."

He continued to kneel in prayer until he began to feel God's peace wash over his soul. He rose and squared his chin. Now was time for action. He strode down the Hill toward Luke and motioned for him to follow.

When Buck passed a berry bush, he pulled off a handful of red berries and continued toward the bunkhouse. There he changed into his buckskin and wrapped a leather band with two eagle feathers around his head. He ground the berries with a mortar and pestle and added just a few drops of water to make a paste before thickening it with bear tallow. Placing two fingers into the paste, Buck scooped enough to draw a thick red line on each cheek and one line from the hairline at the center of his forehead down to the base of his nose.

Buck grabbed the tin of turmeric from the kitchen shelf and repeated the process, adding a bright yellow line beneath each red one on his cheeks. He had chosen the colors purposefully, for red symbolized war and yellow signified grief and mourning. He washed his hands and glanced up at Luke, who was leaning against the doorway.

Luke had never had any reason to fear his Kiowa brother. In this moment, Luke was thankful he was not meeting Buck for the first time. The intensity in Buck's gaze, in combination with the buckskin, eagle feathers, and war paint, made Buck look terrifying. Luke was glad he would never have to meet his brother in battle.

"Come," Buck said to Luke as he exited the bunkhouse.

Tim and the sheriff had just arrived, and Will was getting the details from Emma. Buck walked toward Wind Dancing with purpose, "Will, let's ride."

"Buck, you're not going anywhere. You're way too close to act objectively. The other boys and I will handle this."

Buck turned with a look of determination and fierce intensity. "With all respect, Will, this is my fight, my family, my wife that was nearly beaten to death, my little girl who died. There is no way you're leaving me behind. Besides, I'm the best tracker you have here. You need me. You and my brothers will keep my actions under control."

The sheriff nodded, moved by Buck's passionate speech. "All right, boys, let's ride."

They took off toward the river trail and soon found the area where Julie was beaten. The section of rope used to lasso Julie was still in the dirt. Buck gritted his teeth.

"The footsteps lead back toward the tepee. This way."

When they arrived at the tepee, Buck dismounted and studied the hoof prints.

"Toward the valley. Let's go." They rode down the valley, up the opposite rise, and along the ridge for miles. Finally, the trail led toward a box canyon.

"This is it. We should be able to trap them here."

Will took over. "Luke, you, Tim, and Jacob flank around to the left. James, you and Josiah ride with me to the right. Buck, give us a few minutes to get in position, then ride in to meet them and draw their attention while we surround them. Be careful. We don't want to make Julie a widow today. On my mark. Quietly now. Go."

As Will and the boys expertly wound their way around the sides of the canyon, Buck waited patiently until they were in position. Then he guided Wind Dancing to the mouth of the canyon. When he spotted the gang of men who had forever changed his life, Buck had to consciously check the anger rising inside of him. They were five of the men who had attacked the Sioux hunting party and who later attacked him on Ridge Hill. Their hatred and bitterness had now cost Buck his daughter's life.

With an exterior of perfect calm, Buck called out, "I heard you were looking for me."

The gang leader rose, whisky bottle in one hand, "Looky here, boys, the Indian came to see us. He must've read the calling card we left on the little woman."

Guffawing laughter multiplied as the rest of them rose. "We were just celebrating having one less little Indian to worry about. We're about to get rid of another one. Two in one day. Woohoo!"

About to explode with his anger, Buck clenched his teeth.

He took a deep stabilizing breath, then replied, "The 'little woman' is my wife, and the 'little Indian' you killed today was my daughter."

"He speaks English, too. The woman must be trash to marry the likes of him. He's so stupid, he thought he could come fight us with a war party of one. Haha."

"There is nothing you can say or do to me now that will be worse than what you have already done."

The despicable men started to stagger toward Buck. He raised his bow into the air and let out a war whoop that rang and echoed through the canyon. The men, startled, suddenly realized that horses were coming at them from every direction. The leader raised his gun and shot at Buck, and Buck released an arrow that was true to its mark, straight through the heart. As the leader crumpled to the ground, the other gang members started shooting wildly. Will, Tim, James, and Jacob shot the other four. Soon it was over.

Will called, "Is everyone okay?" He looked around and determined the boys were indeed all right.

"Luke, take Buck home. The rest of us will bury these outlaws."

Buck stopped in front of the ranch house and tied Wind Dancing's reins around the hitching post.

Luke came up beside him. "Buck, go on up and see Julie. I'll take care of Wind Dancing."

"Thank you."

Emma came to the door as Buck approached. Buck answered her unasked question. "It is done. The others will return soon."

"Julie has been asking for you."

Buck climbed the stairs with heavy steps. As he entered the bedroom doorway, Julie extended her hand to him.

"You're safe. Thank you, Lord."

Buck approached and sat on the edge of the bed. "That gang will never hurt our family again."

He looked past her bruises to her soft brown eyes. "I have failed you. I am sorry."

"Buck, none of what happened today was your fault."

"But if I'd been there . . ." Julie raised her finger to his lips.

She repeated, "None of what happened today was your fault. You were exactly where you were supposed to be: on the cattle drive, working alongside your brothers. I was where I was supposed to be: getting our home ready for your return. Those wicked men were the ones who were in the wrong place, doing evil things."

"But if you hadn't married an Indian . . ."

"I didn't marry 'an Indian.' I married you, my Kiowa warrior. And I would marry you again today, for you alone hold my heart. I love you." Julie held her arms to him, and he gently wrapped his around her.

"Oh, my Love, a warrior could not be blessed with a better wife." He held her for many minutes then gradually released her.

"Was our home destroyed?"

"Actually, no. I had not considered it until now, but it seemed undisturbed when we were tracking the gang. I'm surprised they didn't tear it down."

"Finally, something to be thankful for today. Buck, I want to go home."

Buck started to disagree, thinking she would get better care with Emma, but he stopped when he saw the determined look in Julie's eyes.

He nodded instead. "I'll tell Emma."

Buck was only gone a couple of minutes before he returned, gently scooped Julie up in his arms, and carried her down the stairs and out of the house.

The boys were all working around the bunkhouse and corral when Buck exited the house. The brothers who had not yet seen Julie since the violence were horrified as they saw her now.

Tim breathed, "If the men who did this were not already dead, I'd go and kill them myself."

James put a calming hand on Tim's shoulder. The respect for their Kiowa brother rose in their eyes that day, for he had shown control in the midst of the worst of trials.

Buck asked his wife, "Do you want me to take you to the Hill on our way home?"

"Wouldn't that be too far out of the way?"

"Nothing is too far out of the way for you, my Love."

"Then yes, please."

Buck made his way to the new grave, where he carefully set Julie on her feet and took a knee so Julie could sit on his other leg. She wrapped her arms around his neck and sobbed for several minutes. Gradually, the sobs turned to quiet tears. "Thank you," she whispered.

"For what?"

"For creating life with me, for being my strength when I am weak, for loving me when I am unlovely, for having unwavering faith when mine would falter."

"You are confused, my Love. It is you who is my strength."

After a pause, Julie spoke again, "Doc said I may not be able to carry more children."

"Yes, he told me. If that is God's plan, know that I am perfectly content with you and you alone."

"I love you."

Buck rose, lifting Julie into his arms once more, and walked to the river trail that led to their home. Julie was right. It did feel good to be home, just the two of them, away from even well-meaning curious eyes, so healing could begin.

Spring blossomed into summer, then into the colors of autumn. God had restored their joy. Buck and Julie worked together to train Spice, along with several other young horses, finding that their styles of training foals were indeed very similar. This shared passion for horses was just one more way that they were one: one in marriage, one in dreams, one before God. Unless their duties called them apart, Buck and Julie were inseparable. God answered their prayer and brought healing to Julie's womb as well as their hearts. By their first anniversary, Julie was certain she was carrying life once again. She kept her secret, wanting this news to be her Love's Christmas gift.

Chapter 17
Influenza

A few weeks after Buck and Julie's first anniversary, harvest time began in earnest. Since breakfast at the ranch house was the family meeting time to discuss who was working the ranch chores and who was going to the neighboring farms to help harvest crops based on the needs of the day, James asked Buck and Julie to join them at the table. They would ride up together on Wind Dancing at dawn. Julie would help Emma cook and serve breakfast then prepare lunches for the extra workers at the farm being harvested that day. Buck would ride out with his brothers. They all put in long hours this time of year.

The fifth day after harvest began, Josiah came to breakfast with flushed cheeks. He wasn't one to ever complain, but Julie could tell he wasn't feeling well. As she set the bowl of scrambled eggs on the table, she stepped behind Josiah and placed her hand on his forehead.

"Josiah, you are burning up." Julie made eye contact with James as he sat at the head of the table.

James instructed, "Josiah, head back to the bunkhouse and lie down."

Josiah stood and slowly exited the front door. The fact that he did not argue that he could work anyway was proof of his illness. Julie spoke to Emma, then grabbed a bowl, some washrags, and a mason jar of chicken broth and followed him to the bunkhouse.

171

When Julie arrived, she discovered that Josiah had already flopped down on his bunk without so much as taking off his boots. She filled the bowl with cool water and dropped in the washrags. After she set the bowl on the floor by his bunk, she sat on the edge of his bed, wrung out one of the washrags, and began wiping his face with the cool water.

Julie laid the rag across his forehead. "Josiah, let me help you remove your boots."

His only response was a groan.

"Do you hurt anywhere?"

"I hurt everywhere. My head, my throat, my joints. Even my skin hurts."

Julie had remembered feeling that way once when she was young, the time she had come down with influenza. Concern for Josiah furrowed her brow as James came to the bunkhouse doorway to check on him.

Julie requested, "James, could you send someone for the doctor? I think Josiah might have influenza."

Knowing Julie was never one to exaggerate, James replied, "I'll send Tim right away."

An hour later, Doc examined Josiah, "Julie is right. He has influenza. Tim just found me at the Johnson farm. Jeb and his two boys are fighting influenza, too. Did Josiah help with their harvest earlier this week?"

"Yes. Luke and Jacob were there with him," James replied from the doorway.

"I'm sure they probably all shared the same water bucket and ladle. Keep those two at the ranch, and keep a close eye on them. Send them in here if they start showing any symptoms. This bunkhouse is now under quarantine. James, you and Tim need to sleep at the house until these boys are well."

Doc looked up at Julie, "And another thing. Buck cannot enter this bunkhouse for any reason. James, you will need to assign him to the ranch to keep him away from other farmers that may be carrying influenza."

"Why do you have special instructions for Buck?" James wondered.

"The Indians have very little immunity against influenza. I don't know if it's just the way God made them or simply because they have not been exposed to white men's diseases, but what is miserable for you boys would be life-threatening to him. Tell him to sleep and eat in the tepee. I want him to have as little contact as possible with anyone until you are all healthy."

Doc again turned to Julie, "I am sorry to separate you, but this is important."

"I understand," Julie answered.

"Aside from that, I must say you are doing a great job caring for Josiah. I already spotted your hand-washing bucket. That may be the most important, especially when Luke and Jacob come."

"I will be sure they have their own cooling cloths and cups."

"Good girl. I wish all my patients had a nurse as thoughtful as you. By the way, you will need to stay quarantined here, too."

"I had assumed as much. I'll sleep on Buck's bunk."

"Be sure you do. Having had influenza does give you more immunity than anyone else here at the ranch, but it is not a guarantee you will not get it. Proper rest will help guard you from getting sick."

While Doc was instructing Julie, Luke approached the doorway. Julie took one look at his flushed face and spoke, "Luke, take off your boots and lie down."

"I feel like I've been run over by a horse," he said as he slipped off his boots.

Julie washed her hands before feeling his forehead. "Doc, he's burning up, too."

"Unless I miss my guess, Jacob will be soon behind him. Julie, here is some medicine to stir into their water cups to help with the fever and aches. Use one teaspoon twice a day."

"Yes, sir. I'll take good care of them," replied Julie.

Doc placed a hand on her shoulder, "I know you will. I will be back to check on you tomorrow. If you need me before then, send Tim or James for me."

As Doc exited the bunkhouse, he spotted Jacob walking slowly across the barnyard. "Jacob, head into the bunkhouse. Julie is waiting for you." James was standing near Doc's horse. "That's three for three. Pray none of the rest of you get sick. Keep the four of them quarantined until I clear them. Do you understand?"

"Yes, I understand." James paused before asking, "Are the three of them going to be all right?"

"They are young and strong, and they have their own personal nurse. We quarantined them early. Now we just have to let the influenza run its course. I give them a good chance of complete recovery, but I don't want to minimize the disease they are fighting. I'm so thankful Buck wasn't on that farm team this week."

"Me, too," James agreed.

Just then, Buck walked up. James addressed their doctor, "Doc, explain to Buck what you told Julie."

Buck had a sober expression as he listened to Doc's instructions. He informed Doc, "I am half white."

"That may be, but you certainly look Indian, and for now, we're going under the assumption that your level of immunity comes from your Indian fathers. To take unnecessary chances would be foolish. Hopefully, by next week, you may again hold your wife."

Buck looked at James as he addressed Doc, "I will abide by your instructions."

James delegated, "You stay here at the ranch and cover the ranch chores. Tim and I will ride out to the Wilson's farm to lend a hand."

Buck nodded and turned to walk to the barn to saddle Wind Dancing. He would start with inspecting the perimeter fences and checking on the herd. This was going to be a lonely week.

After his ride, Buck pulled Wind Dancing to a stop in front of the bunkhouse. He called to Julie, and she came to the doorway. "Are you all right, my Love?"

"Yes, I am all right, but these boys are miserable. All three are burning up with fever, and Luke lost his breakfast."

Buck crinkled his face in a way that made Julie laugh.

"Did Doc or James speak to you about the quarantine?"

"Yes, they both spoke to me." Buck switched to Kiowa, *"My isolation has just begun, and my arms already ache to hold you."*

Julie smiled, *"Being in your arms is my favorite place to be, but my love for you is too great not to protect you from this illness."*

Buck nodded his understanding. *"Is there anything you need from the tepee?"*

"If you could bring my nightdress and a second change of clothes, that would be very helpful. Just leave the bundle on the porch and I'll get it."

"Where will you sleep tonight?" Buck wondered.

"In your bunk. Your pillow still smells like you."

Buck smiled, *"I love you."*

"I love you." Julie waved good-bye and watched as Buck turned and guided Wind Dancing toward the corral.

When Doc came by the second day, he was pleased with their condition. Julie was surprised, since none of their fevers had broken. He explained, "One of the greatest dangers initially is severe dehydration. You are preventing that by having them sip water regularly. Giving them the medicine and wiping their faces and chests with the cool water helps them to rest more comfortably, so their bodies can fight the influenza more effectively. I would expect that their fevers should start breaking in the next 24 to 48 hours." He added with a smile, "Keep in mind that they will probably get grumpy and harder to mother when they start feeling better. Put on your stern face and keep them in line." Julie laughed. "How are you feeling?"

"So far, so good, other than missing Buck like crazy."

Now it was Doc's turn to smile. "Hang in there. These three boys are lucky to have you. I'll be back tomorrow."

"Would you ask Buck to bring a bucket of fresh water to the porch? I'm nearly out."

"You bet." Doc washed his hands and exited the bunkhouse.

Early the next morning, Luke's fever broke, and he drenched his bed with sweat. Julie wiped his face and smiled; she felt a cool forehead for about an hour before Luke's teeth started chattering and his fever climbed once more. Jacob's and Josiah's fevers broke just before lunch. All three were running fevers again by the time Doc came by, but he was encouraged that all of them had broken their fevers at least once.

Julie had her hands full. When the fevers would break, she would feed them broth and buttered toast and make sure they drank water. When shivering and teeth chattering began as the fevers spiked, she would bathe their faces and chests with the cool water so they could rest. They were getting more ornery, but Julie took this as a good sign that they were starting to feel better.

On the fifth morning, Luke was sitting on the side of his bed eating the first real breakfast in what seemed to him like forever. When he glanced up at Julie to say "Thank you," he realized she wasn't smiling. That was so out of character for her that he looked more closely at her face.

"Uh-oh. Julie, are you feeling all right?"

"Honestly, I'm not sure," Julie replied.

Luke stood and put his hand on her flushed face. Her skin was hot.

"Now it's my turn to take care of you."

He grabbed the pillow from Buck's bunk and exchanged it with the one on James' bed below.

"Lie down."

She tried to protest, "That's not necessary. I'm probably just tired."

"Julie, look at me and tell me you're not feeling feverish, achy, or just plain miserable."

She looked at him, but remained silent. Instead, a solitary tear escaped down her cheek.

He added gently, "That's what I thought. Go ahead and lie down. I'm not taking no for an answer."

He pointed to the lower bed.

Her fever and headache were getting the better of her. Her thoughts were getting foggy. "But that is James' bed."

Luke smiled at her comment. "Yes, I know who sleeps there, but you do not need to be climbing in and out of a top bunk when you're weaker tomorrow. I swapped pillows so you could sleep on Buck's."

"All right" were her only other words before she all but collapsed into the lower bunk.

Julie had been meticulous about making sure he and his brothers had their own cups and cooling cloths to prevent the further spread of infection, but now Luke had no additional supplies for Julie. When he had once assisted Doc in a surgery, Doc had explained how he boiled his instruments to kill any germs. He would do the same thing. He put a pot of water on to boil and collected his things. After they had been in the boiling water for several minutes, he removed his cup, bowl, and cloths with tongs and laid them on the counter to cool.

Luke looked over at Jacob and Josiah. They were both still sleeping, but they were starting to stir, and would be up soon. Breakfast was still warm, and he knew they would enjoy it as much as he had. The hardest part of this day was going to be telling Buck that Julie was now ill because she had cared for him and his brothers.

An hour later, while Jacob and Josiah were eating their breakfast and Julie was sleeping with a cool cloth on her forehead, Buck called Julie's name. Luke took a deep breath and went to the doorway.

"Where's Julie?" Buck wanted to know.

"Buck, Julie started running a fever this morning. She looks pretty miserable, but she's finally asleep now. I'm guessing she caught influenza from us."

Buck strode toward the bunkhouse and made it up two steps before Luke held up his hand and spoke firmly, "Stop!"

Luke so seldom spoke forcibly to anyone, that Buck froze on the second step. Buck explained, "She is my wife. I should be the one to take care of her."

Luke wasn't going to lose this fight. "Not this time, Buck. You gave your word that you would not enter this bunkhouse until the quarantine was lifted. Besides, Julie would never forgive me if I let you in and you contracted influenza from her."

Buck backed down the two steps, ran his fingers through his hair, and paced back and forth in front of the stairs. "I so want to be with her."

Luke had never seen Buck act this way. "I know how much you love Julie, but who would care for her if you died from influenza?" Luke asked quietly. Buck folded his arms and looked heavenward, obviously trying to control his emotions. "Listen, Doc has been coming mid-afternoon. Why don't you ride the perimeter this morning and do barn chores after lunch? That way, you will be close by when Doc comes, and you can get an update directly from him."

Knowing Luke was trying to help, Buck nodded. "Is there anything you need before I ride out?"

"Not that I know of. Julie had us well-supplied in here."

Buck nodded again, then turned to walk to the corral for Wind Dancing. Luke breathed a sigh of relief. He never enjoyed confrontation, but standing up to this big brother that he loved and admired took more courage than he thought he possessed. The truth was, he was concerned about Julie, too. He and his brothers had made it through their illness, but Julie was so petite and fragile. He just hoped she was stronger than she looked.

When Luke turned back into the bunkhouse, Jacob commented, "I'm glad I didn't have to have that conversation with Buck. Julie looks awful."

"I'm sure that's how we looked a couple of days ago. Do either of you know how much medicine she gave us?" When Josiah and Jacob shook their heads, Luke continued, "I'm not sure either. I'll wait and ask Doc when he comes."

Over the next couple of hours, he continued to wipe her face with the cool damp cloths, but her fever seemed to be getting higher. She became too delirious to drink anything.

Luke wanted to send for Doc, but he had sent Buck on a perimeter ride. There would be no one else here at the ranch. Just when he was about to ask Jacob to break quarantine and ride out for the doctor, Luke heard Doc's buggy pull up in front of the bunkhouse. He breathed, "Thank you, Lord."

Doc stepped up onto the porch and smiled when he saw Josiah. "Well, you look like you're feeling better."

"Yes, sir, but Julie isn't," Josiah answered.

Doc entered and followed Josiah's gaze to where Luke was sitting on the edge of Julie's bed.

Luke gave him the update. "She started spiking a fever this morning. I can't get her to drink any water, and she just keeps getting hotter."

Julie started thrashing in the bed.

"Step aside, son." Luke moved away so Doc could do his assessment. "Julie's heart is racing, and her fever is too high. We've got to get her cooled down now. Fill the tub with cool water. Where is your ice house?"

Jacob answered, "The ice box is in the cellar."

"Jacob, have you run any fever since I saw you yesterday?"

"No, sir. None of us have except Julie."

"Wash your hands and go get a block of ice the size of a small box."

He showed the size with his hands about a foot by six inches. Jacob washed his hands and left immediately. Josiah slid the tub over near Julie and poured in the two buckets of water they had.

"Josiah, wash your hands and get two more buckets of water."

"Luke, lift Julie into the tub, dress and all."

He scooped her up into his arms and set her carefully in the tub. Jacob and Josiah arrived together. Jacob handed Doc the block of ice and helped Josiah by pouring in his second bucket of water. She was immersed up to her chin. Doc laid the ice across Julie's abdomen, then scooped some of the water to dampen the hair on the top of her head.

Buck spotted Doc's buggy entering the ranch and now dismounted Wind Dancing in front of the bunkhouse. As the minutes passed, his concern grew. When worry tempted to take root, he chose rather to voice his thoughts to his Lord. He prayed that his wife would have the strength to fight and win her battle with influenza, and that Doc and Luke would have the wisdom to make the best decisions for her care. Buck knew that while he could not be in the bunkhouse, his God was already there.

Inside, Doc was instructing Luke as they knelt on either side of the tub.

"There is a fine line between lowering a fever out of the danger zone and cooling so much the patient starts to shiver. A fever that is too high can lead to seizures and severe dehydration. Causing the patient to shiver will generate more body heat and raise the fever even further. Some fever is necessary to kill the infection."

"Notice the redness in Julie's cheeks has lessened, and her thrashing has completely stopped. Her heart rate is still higher than normal, which is consistent with fever, infection, and dehydration, but it has slowed significantly from when I arrived."

Julie shifted slightly.

Luke asked, "Julie, are you all right?"

181

He reached out to feel her forehead. It was still warm, but not burning hot as it had been.

Julie opened groggy eyes and looked up into Luke's face, "I feel like I'm swimming."

She took in her surroundings.

"I am swimming. What happened?"

"Your fever went dangerously high. You scared me to death. Thankfully, Doc arrived at just the right time."

She looked over to the man on her other side, "Hi, Dr. Mason. Thanks for coming." She licked her dry lips. "I'm getting cold."

Doc addressed Luke, "That's your cue."

Luke delegated, "Josiah, grab the blanket off Buck's bed and get a couple of towels. Jacob, put this ice in the bunkhouse cold storage in case we need it again. Julie, could you stand if I help you?"

"Yes, I think so."

"Be sure you have a firm hold of her, son. She will be weak," instructed Doc.

Luke ensured he had good footing and held her upper arms. She grasped his forearms. "All right, Julie, slow and easy." He pulled her slowly to standing, and she stepped out of the tub.

"Luke, I'm getting dizzy."

He looked at her face, which had turned pale white. As she began to crumple, he lifted her in his arms.

Luke directed, "Lay the towels on James' bed." Josiah did so. Luke laid Julie down on the towels, reached for the blanket, and tucked it snugly around her.

"Good work, Luke. I couldn't have done that better myself." Doc was pleased.

"Why did she pass out?" Luke wanted to know.

"She's very dehydrated after that fever. Getting her to drink water is now your first priority. Give her some broth, too. The salt in the broth will help her body retain the water. Do you have any medicine left?"

"Yes, sir, but I wasn't sure how much to give, so I waited until I could ask you."

"Mix one teaspoon in her water cup twice a day."

After Luke measured the medicine and stirred it into her cup, he sat on the edge of Julie's bed. She regained consciousness a minute later.

"My head's fuzzy."

"All the more reason you need to drink some of this water for me."

Luke lifted her head and helped her hold the cup while she sipped the cool liquid.

"You and I are going to be buddies today."

"I'm sorry I'm so much trouble."

Julie's voice was made raspy by her sore throat. Luke smiled. She was sweet even when she was sick. Buck was a lucky man.

Luke reassured her, "You are no trouble at all. You cared for us and nursed us back to health. Now it's our turn."

Doc gathered his things. "Julie, I leave you in capable hands. Luke, you shouldn't need to immerse her in ice water again, but leave the tub handy just in case. When she is stronger, bring the privacy screen over and let her change into something dry."

"Yes, sir," Luke responded.

"Boys, I want you to stay quarantined for now since you have all been exposed to Julie today. You should be out of the woods, but I don't want to take any chances, especially with Buck on the ranch."

Jacob addressed Josiah, "Sounds like we need to get out the checker board."

Doc smiled, "See you tomorrow." He exited the bunkhouse. At the bottom of the stairs, Buck stood with folded arms and a solemn expression.

"How is Julie?" Buck needed to know.

Doc expected nothing less than his direct question. "Julie spiked an extremely high fever, causing rather significant dehydration."

Buck's face showed his concern, but Doc was quick to add, "We submerged her in an ice bath to bring down her fever, and she is able to drink fluids again. I think she is past the danger at this point, but Luke knows what to do if her fever climbs too high. Once her fever breaks for a little while, we'll know she's on the mend."

Doc put his hand on Buck's shoulder, "Luke is taking very good care of Julie. Trust him."

"Thank you, Doc."

As he climbed into his buggy, Doc reminded Buck, "The bunkhouse is still under quarantine until Julie is well. Stay away, young man."

Buck nodded.

Later that night, Julie's fever finally broke, and Luke breathed a sigh of relief. When Buck came by for another update before heading home to sleep in the tepee, Luke was able to share the good news.

"Is Julie asleep?" Buck asked.

"No, but she's still too weak to stand for long," Luke replied.

Buck lifted his voice in the Kiowa tongue, *"My Love, I am very happy to hear your fever has broken. My heart and my prayers are with you. I long for the moment when you will come to me again. My arms are lonely."*

Luke looked over at Julie as she spoke, then he addressed Buck with a chuckle. "She said something I

184

couldn't understand and am afraid to try to repeat, but her expression is as close to a smile as I've seen all day."

"Rest well, my Wife. I love you."

Luke listened to Julie and told Buck, "She repeated your last phrase."

Buck smiled and nodded. Before he turned to leave, he added, "Thank you, Luke, for caring for Julie when I cannot."

"You're welcome." When he turned away from the doorway to check on Julie, Luke noticed she was starting to have chills again as her fever climbed once more. He sat on the edge of Julie's bed and bathed her face with cool water.

Julie confided in Luke, "I'm so glad I was able to hear Buck's voice. I miss him so much."

"He misses you, too. It was all I could do to keep him out of the bunkhouse this morning. Standing up to him was probably the hardest thing I've ever done."

"You really admire him," recognized Julie.

"Yes, I do. Of all my brothers, he is the one I wish to be most like."

"Why?"

"Well, for one thing, I think our personalities are fairly similar. I look up to him for many reasons. He is a man of his word. He never misses the details. He thoughtfully considers everything he does. This morning was the only time I have ever known him to be the least bit impulsive. He is never afraid to stand for what is right. He is the strongest of all of us, but he may be the most gentle, too. The gentleness I had seen from him with the animals is only magnified in the way he treats you. He has endured tragedy and has continued to face injustice, yet his kindness and his faith never waver. And he has a beautiful wife who loves him very much."

"You are more like him than you realize, though you couldn't look more different with your fair skin, blond hair, and blue eyes. For you, observing the details and being thoughtful and gentle is what makes you a good doctor to the animals and to me. You had the courage to stand up to Buck and preserve the quarantine, not because it was easy, but because it was right. As for a wife, God has a sweet young lady out there somewhere for you. When you find her in His perfect timing, she will be blessed to have a man like you for a husband."

"Thank you, Julie."

After she drank some more water and broth, she dozed off. Luke kept a close eye on her, but the fever did not rise to the dangerous level as before. Her fever cycled through chills and sweats throughout the night and the next morning, but by afternoon, her fever was gone for good and her other symptoms started to improve.

Finally, on the seventh day, Julie and the boys had been fever-free for twenty-four hours when Doc came by and proclaimed them restored to health. With the stipulation that their clothes and all the sheets would be washed and bunkhouse cleaned before anyone else could enter, he ended the quarantine. The boys were so ready to be out of the bunkhouse that they helped her with the cleaning and laundry.

Buck had brought Julie a fresh change of clothes. Once she slipped behind the privacy screen and changed into her clean dress, she all but ran out the front door and into Buck's arms. Buck smiled as he held her close. He glanced up to see his brothers all smiling at him. He turned with Julie until his back was to his brothers and bent his head to kiss her. When Jacob whistled, Buck touched Julie's forehead with his, and Julie laughed. He asked his wife, "Do you mind my kissing you in front of my brothers?"

"Not at all." That was the only invitation he needed to kiss her again.

Chapter 18
The Epidemic

A few weeks later, harvest was done throughout Prairie Hills. No one had to wonder if Buck would take Julie to the annual church social this year. So much had changed since this event two years ago, yet some things remained the same. Julie wore the same cream-colored dress, for it was Buck's favorite. He borrowed the buggy, and lifted Julie onto the seat, not because he needed to lift her now that she could see, but because he loved the closeness he shared with her when he showed her this special kindness. He climbed in the other side, and she scooted close to him. Buck smiled as he leaned toward Julie and kissed her. Soon they were off. Buck was proud to have Julie dancing in his arms all evening. The evening was delightful.

When they returned to the ranch, Buck unhitched the horse and parked the buggy while Julie led the horse to the barn and settled him in his stall. Buck and Julie walked together hand in hand toward their buffalo skin home. The sky was clear with a million pinpoints of light. Buck looked down at Julie and spoke, "I was thinking."

"Yes?"

Buck smiled, "The buffalo herd will move further south soon, and your village will follow and not return until late spring or summer. Since the warm weather is holding, would you like to take a ride to your village before winter sets in?"

"Oh, yes, that would be wonderful!" Julie exclaimed.

"Then it is settled. We will leave on Monday morning, and plan to return Tuesday evening."

On Monday morning, Running Buck and Desert Rose dressed in their buckskin. Desert Rose made a point to remember to wear her gifted moccasins and the necklace White Feather had given her as a wedding gift. They mounted Wind Dancing, with Desert Rose riding behind her husband, her arms circled around him and her cheek against his back. Buck couldn't help but smile. The fall weather was cool in the mornings and evenings but still delightfully warm in the afternoons. When they stopped for their noon meal, Buck leaned his back against the trunk of an oak tree and his wife leaned against his shoulder. Buck put his arm around her and smiled, "This trip will be much more pleasant for me than the last."

"Yes, no warrior can leave a gift for me, for this time I am a wife."

"This time you are my wife." He kissed her.

"Where will we sleep?" she wondered.

"We are the family of White Feather and Runs Like the Wind. They will ask us to stay with them. Is there enough room in your bed for two?"

Desert Rose smiled as she teased, "Hmm. It might be a little snug, but I think I can make room for you." A sudden thought occurred to her, "Will I now be allowed to speak to you in public?"

"Of course. I will also be permitted to speak directly to you, walk with you, eat with you, and enter a tepee with you. Being married affords us many privileges."

"What will the warriors who asked your consent to leave me a gift think when I enter the village as your wife?" Desert Rose asked.

"That I am the most blessed warrior in the village," Running Buck replied. "Come. Let us finish our journey." They remounted Wind Dancing and rode the remaining distance to the village.

This time his greeting was slightly different. Runs Like the Wind was the primary sentry on duty. *"Hello, Runs Like the Wind. My wife and I would like to request lodging tonight so Desert Rose and I may visit with you and White Feather."*

The eyes of Runs Like the Wind sparkled. *"My son, we would be honored. You and your wife may enter our village."*

Running Buck replied with a smile, *"Many thanks."*

Desert Rose stayed with Running Buck as he unsaddled Wind Dancing and released him in the corral.

"Come. Let us find White Feather."

On their way, Morning Song ran after her son White Fox and nearly ran right into Desert Rose. Running Buck scooped up the little boy as he tried to run past and held him for a moment while Morning Song caught her breath and hugged her friend. Suddenly, Morning Song realized Desert Rose and Running Buck were walking together. She held her friend at arms length, glanced briefly at Running Buck, and asked, *"Are you now a wife?"*

Desert Rose smiled, *"Yes, I am the wife of Running Buck."*

Morning Song grinned, *"May you know much happiness and bear many sons."* She added with a laugh, *"Though sons will steal your energy and leave you tired."*

She reached to take White Fox from Running Buck. *"Have you seen White Feather yet?"*

"No, not yet."

"Then go."

Morning Song gave her one more quick hug and turned to take her son back to her home.

Desert Rose and Running Buck found White Feather sitting in front of her tepee, weaving a basket. When White

Feather looked up and saw them, her smiling eyes quickly took in the necklace and moccasins Desert Rose was wearing. She stood and embraced her daughter.

"You are a wife. My heart overflows with joy." She looked at Running Buck, *"Welcome to our family, my son."*

"Many thanks, White Feather."

When dinnertime came, Running Buck and Desert Rose ate together first as guests. While Runs Like the Wind and White Feather ate, Running Buck and Desert Rose entered the tepee together. Knowing they had only a few minutes before his wife's parents joined them, Running Buck embraced his wife, who tipped her face up toward his, and he kissed her.

Runs Like the Wind and White Feather entered the tepee a few minutes later. Desert Rose and Running Buck sat together on the edge of her bed, and he reached for her hand and held it gently in his. Desert Rose told them about their wedding and the tepee that Running Buck had built for their home. With sadness and a few tears, they told her parents about the death of their granddaughter. Running Buck spoke with pride about her caring for his brothers as they fought influenza and won their fight, only to catch influenza herself and win her fight.

Desert Rose caught Buck looking up through the opening in the tepee. As she looked up, she saw the sunset. When her eyes met Buck's, they both smiled. On this night, he hadn't needed to excuse himself before sunset. As her husband, he could stay with her.

Runs Like the Wind noticed the exchange and wrapped his arm around White Feather. She was smiling, for she had seen it, too. Their daughter was not only a wife, she was also very much in love.

When Runs Like the Wind asked, Running Buck pulled out their Bible, and he read to them, translated for them, and prayed with them. Soon the time for sleep arrived. Runs Like The Wind offered to let Running Buck and Desert Rose have their bed, while White Feather slept in their daughter's bed, and he slept on the ground, but they politely refused. Desert Rose's bed was rather narrow, but when Running Buck laid down on his side, there was just enough room for his wife. Runs Like the Wind started to protest, but White Feather stopped him.

"We were young once. Leave them be."

Desert Rose lay down on her side in front of Buck. He covered both of them with the fur blanket and wrapped his arm around his wife so she wouldn't fall off the edge. When they snuggled together under the fur blanket, they were actually quite comfortable. Against her back, she could feel Buck's breathing even out in the soft rhythm of sleep. She smiled and soon joined him in peaceful rest. God gave them both a good night's sleep, for He alone knew what the next day would bring.

The next morning, as Running Buck and Desert Rose were eating breakfast at the family fire, Desert Rose noticed a warrior slowly staggering toward the campfires. Her brow furrowed in concern as she leaned toward her husband and spoke softly in English, "Buck, I have a bad feeling about him. That's exactly the way the boys looked on their worst day with influenza."

Just then, the man collapsed.

"I will ask my father to get Hunting Owl, the medicine man."

Desert Rose stood and walked over to address her father. *"Have any traders come to the village in the last few days?"*

"Yes," he replied.

"Did any of them appear to be ill?" she queried.

193

"Actually, one of them seemed rather tired and grumpy. He kept complaining of a headache."

"Did Prowling Bear have any contact with him?" she continued to ply him with questions.

"Yes, he was part of the trading council. Why the questions?"

"Prowling Bear now looks like my brothers did when they were fighting influenza. If I am right, he needs to be quarantined right away. Would you ask Hunting Owl to examine him?"

Running Buck waited while Prowling Bear was assessed, spoke quietly to the medicine man, and sought to address the Chief. In a few minutes, Chief Soaring Eagle came to Desert Rose.

"Come and stand before me."

Not knowing that Buck had requested an audience with him, she feared she had done something wrong. Nevertheless, Desert Rose stood before the chief and kept her eyes respectfully to the ground.

"Desert Rose, Running Buck and Hunting Owl tell me our brother suffers from influenza. Since you have recently cared for your brothers, Hunting Owl is requesting your help. Influenza nearly wiped out a neighboring village last month and must be dealt with seriously. For this time, you have my permission to speak directly to anyone in the village and to care for our people in whatever way you must. Tell my people what you need, and it will be done." He was removing the cultural barriers to their care and giving her much freedom in the village, but he was also placing a heavy weight of responsibility on her shoulders.

"May I ask two questions of the Chief?" Desert Rose asked timidly.

"Yes," he responded simply.

"First, may we send for the white medicine man to bring special medicine to the village?"

"Yes. What is your second question?"

"*Influenza is easily spread from one person to another. Though Prowling Bear is now under quarantine, we do not know whom our brother has been near since he became ill. May the Chief ask our people to stay within their tepees and come out only when absolutely necessary? Containing this disease is very important.*"

"*Let it be done.*" Chief Soaring Eagle turned and left, signifying the meeting was over.

Desert Rose turned to see Buck making his way toward her, and she closed distance between them.

He spoke in English, "Who knew my wife would become the acting Chief of her village?"

"Don't tease me. This is a huge burden of responsibility. Some of my people will die, and I will be blamed."

"The chief knows you are their only hope. He will not falsely accuse you. I did not mean to tease, for I am proud of you. What do you need me to do?"

Desert Rose took a deep, steady breath and exhaled. "I hesitate to ask you to ride so many miles, but I need you and Wind Dancing to get medicine from Dr. Mason and to bring him back with you, if you can."

"Do not hesitate to ask. You are under the chief's authority. Ask firmly what you need. The warriors will respond better to you that way."

Desert Rose nodded.

"I will leave now for the medicine, but I will not make it back tonight. Will you be all right until noon tomorrow?"

"I have no other choice. Be safe. Pray as you ride. Pray that God will give me wisdom and give them the strength to fight this disease."

"I will. I love you, my Wife."

"I love you, my Warrior."

Running Buck turned toward the corral to get Wind Dancing for the ride home. Desert Rose prayed for courage and confidence as she sought the medicine man. He had the look of fear in his eyes. She tried to be bold.

"Hunting Owl, we must be sure no one visits the tepee of Prowling Bear. We will place a bucket at the door to wash our hands every time we go in or out. He must have his own cup and cooling rag, even if others get sick and join him in his tepee. Right now, we must encourage him to drink as much water as possible. I will go from tepee to tepee, asking everyone to stay inside unless they start showing signs of the illness."

"When the white medicine man's medicine arrives, it will help lower the fever and lessen the pain. Until then, do you have some lavender oils and clove to help him rest and clean the air?"

He nodded and soon returned with tiny bottles of lavender and clove.

Needing to know who else might have been exposed to the sick trader, Desert Rose returned to her parents' tepee and asked her father, *"Who else was part of the trading council with the sick man?"*

"Gray Wolf and I." That her father had been so closely exposed shook her, but she determined to remain composed.

"If you begin running a fever or developing a severe headache or joint aches, please come to the tepee of Prowling Bear right away," she instructed.

Runs Like the Wind nodded solemnly.

"I pray you will stay well. I must see Gray Wolf."

Praying that God would spare her father from succumbing to influenza, Desert Rose crossed the village with heavy steps. She stood before the tepee of Gray Wolf and called, *"Gray Wolf, I need to speak with you."* To speak so boldly in the village felt unnatural, but this was necessary.

Gray Wolf soon exited the tepee. *"Yes?"*

Standing before her was the man who had first left a gift for her just after she turned fifteen. Now she addressed him as another warrior's wife.

"Gray Wolf, the sick trader you met a few days ago is likely the source of Prowling Bear's influenza. Since you were also in the trading council, you may also have been exposed. If you begin feeling ill, please come see me or Hunting Owl right away. To delay would mean putting your family at risk." Gray Wolf nodded and reentered his tepee.

As Desert Rose turned to make her way back to Prowling Bear, she whispered, "Lord, please protect the people of my village." She cared for Prowling Bear as she had cared for her brothers, cooling his fevered face with cool water and giving him as much water and broth as he could tolerate. A few hours later, he was still her only patient, and he seemed to be stable.

"If he is the only one who becomes ill, we are truly blessed," she prayed quietly.

Just as the sun dipped below the horizon, Desert Rose heard someone call her name. Her heart sank as she recognized the voice of Runs Like the Wind. She opened the tepee flap and was greeted by the chilly evening air. After she washed her hands, she performed a forbidden gesture and placed her hand on his forehead. He was definitely running a fever. The fact that he did not even flinch when she touched his face proved how ill he felt.

"Come in and lie down, Father. You need rest and water."

Her father asked hesitantly, *"Is Prowling Bear dead?"*

"No, he is sleeping. Though he still runs a fever, he is doing all right so far. Why do you ask?"

Runs Like the Wind visibly relaxed. *"Those in the village are calling this tepee 'The Tepee of Death.'"*

"I had forgotten how superstitious our people can be when illness is involved. Have you heard if any others are getting sick?" Desert Rose asked.

"There are rumors that Gray Wolf and Snow Hare are sick, but I do not know for sure," her father answered.

"Let's get you comfortable, then I will send Hunting Owl to check on them."

As she awaited word from Hunting Owl, she bathed her father's face and encouraged him to drink some water and broth. "When Running Buck arrives tomorrow, he will have medicine that will ease the fever and the aches. Until then, let me rub some lavender oil on your chest to help you rest."

Desert Rose heard a commotion outside and excused herself to wash her hands and exit the tepee. Night had fallen, and the chill in the air seemed to enhance the fear in the village. Hunting Owl was arguing with Gray Wolf, and the discussion became so heated that the chief himself stepped in to order his son to the quarantine tepee. Gray Wolf was adamant, "I will not go to the tepee of death."

Hunting Owl assured him, "If you do not go, you will bring death to your family." Finally, the words of his father the chief brought him reluctantly to Desert Rose.

With her heart beating thuds in her chest, Desert Rose raised her voice enough to be heard by most of the village, "This is not the tepee of death. It is the tepee of sickness. If we can contain the sickness to this buffalo skin, this tepee will become the tepee of life to everyone who is protected from influenza. We must work together to isolate those who are ill to protect those who are weak, especially the elderly and very young. Do not share cups, and wash your hands often. Please do not be afraid to meet me or Hunting Owl if you are getting sick. Prowling Bear and Runs Like the Wind are doing all right so far, and we pray they are strong enough to win their fight. Please do not let your fears lead to foolish decisions."

She entered the tepee and checked on her patients. Prowling Bear was still sleeping, so she went to her father.

"I am so proud of you, my daughter. You spoke like the Chief himself. I hope our people listen."

"As do I, for their very lives depend on it."

Just then, Gray Wolf entered.

"Come. Lie down here."

She washed her hands again and felt his forehead. He glared at her, but he, too, was burning with fever.

She laid a cool cloth across his forehead, which he promptly removed. She got him his own water cup, which he knocked out of her hands.

"I will not be treated like an invalid."

"Gray Wolf, you have shown enough stubbornness tonight. I understand that you are angry and afraid, but I am here to help you. Keeping your face cool will help you to rest better, and the water is necessary to minimize the effects of the fever. I wish for the husband of Morning Song to live through this. Let me take care of you."

The fire slowly left his eyes, and he finally nodded and accepted the water cup.

By morning, five more had come, and a second tepee had been designated for the quarantine. When Desert Rose entered the first tepee, Runs Like the Wind was awake and saw her tears, *"What is it, my daughter?"*

"Snow Hare just died."

"She was old," commented Gray Wolf.

"That may be, but she was a friend, and she will be missed." She addressed her father, *"She was just too weak to fight."*

Runs Like the Wind laid his hand on her head as she knelt by his bed, *"Do not be discouraged, you are helping many."*

"Many thanks, Father. When Running Buck arrives with the medicine, perhaps these stubborn fevers will start breaking."

When Desert Rose ducked out of the tepee to check on her other patients, a chilly gust of wind caught her attention. As she looked up, the dark, menacing clouds rolling in seemed cast a shadow on her heart. She had been counting on the medicine, but Buck would not be able to ride in the storm that was sure to descend upon them at any time.

"Lord, my village needs that medicine. Please calm the storm so Buck can come."

As if in answer, at that very moment, the lightning flashed and the thunder crashed as the downpour began. "Lord, give me strength to endure, and give me wisdom to care for these people until Buck returns."

The storm lasted all morning and all afternoon, finally abating just before the sunset that glowed a brilliant red. Desert Rose breathed a sigh of relief. A red sky in the evening meant clear weather tomorrow. Unfortunately, the temperature was really beginning to drop. The warm fall had disappeared.

About an hour after nightfall, Desert Rose heard her name from just outside the second tepee. She slipped through the opening to find Morning Song standing there with tears streaming down her face. In her arms was her infant son, Coyote.

"Morning Song, no!" Desert Rose lifted a hand to his face. He was burning with fever and taking little gasping breaths.

"Has he been able to drink any milk?"

Morning Song simply shook her head.

"Are you ill?"

She shook her head again.

"Then I don't want you in the quarantine tepee with the others. Sit here." She indicated a short stool just outside the tepee.

Desert Rose ducked in to retrieve some lavender oil and a cool, wet cloth. She wiped his face and chest, applied a tiny amount of oil to his chest, hoping it might ease his breathing a bit.

When the little boy seemed to relax, Desert Rose suggested, *"See if he might nurse now. He needs the water in the milk."*

Morning Song tried, but he was just too weak to nurse.

Desert Rose was torn about what to do. She didn't want to keep Morning Song and her sick baby in the chilly night air, but she didn't want to expose Morning Song to those quarantined in the warm tepee, either. In the end, she didn't need to choose. As Desert Rose joined her friend in tears for this little life, Coyote took his final breath on earth and entered heaven's gates.

The two sobbed together for several minutes before Morning Song asked, *"Could Gray Wolf see him one last time?"*

Desert Rose nodded, *"Of course."* She took the little bundle from Morning Song and carried it into the first tepee. Gray Wolf turned his face toward her as she entered and came to kneel in front of his bed. He saw first the tears coursing down her cheeks, then he recognized the blanket.

"Coyote has now soared from this earth to the Great Spirit."

Gray Wolf shifted to his side so he could see the face of his son. As he reached out to touch him, the strong warrior began to cry.

Several minutes passed while Desert Rose waited patiently for him to grieve his loss. Finally, he spoke with a voice made raspy with emotion, *"If only I had come sooner, he might still be alive."*

"Gray Wolf, you cannot blame yourself. He may have been exposed before you began having signs of illness. Keep your strength so that you may win this fight. Morning Song needs you to comfort her and grieve with her."

He bent over the bed and kissed Coyote's cheek, then looked up at Desert Rose. *"Many thanks."*

She lifted the little boy and carried him back to his mother. *"Gray Wolf grieves with you. He shed tears of sadness and kissed Coyote on the cheek. Morning Song, my heart aches for you."*

Morning Song stood, hugged Desert Rose again, and left her son in Desert Rose's arms saying, *"I do not wish White Fox to get the sickness from Coyote."* Morning Song returned to her tepee with sorrowful steps and empty arms.

Desert Rose shivered in the night air as she took the steps to White Feather's tepee.

"White Feather, are you well?" Her mother peered through the tepee's flap with fearful eyes.

"Do not worry, Father is resting well. I am hoping his fever will break soon."

A visible weight was lifted from her. *"Then what is it that brings you out in the cold, my daughter?"*

"May I please have the lidded basket for Coyote?"

White Feather suddenly noticed the bundle Desert Rose was holding. Tears filled her eyes. *"My prayers are with Morning Song tonight. Here is the basket."*

"Many thanks, Mother. Stay well." Desert Rose placed Coyote gently in the basket, fitted the lid, and carried him back to the first tepee. There she tucked the basket just inside the entrance. She was shivering as much from the emotion of the last hour as from the cold, but as her father had reminded her earlier, she couldn't forget to care for those still living. She washed her hands and arms and began checking her patients.

None of the fevers had broken yet, but Prowling Bear and Runs Like the Wind definitely seemed to be resting more comfortably. Gray Wolf had turned to face the wall of the tepee, and she could hear him softly weeping. She would not disturb him now. She grabbed a buckskin robe before exiting to check on the second tepee. When Desert Rose stepped outside into the cold wind, she shivered and pulled the robe more tightly around her.

The four in the second tepee seemed stable, too. Three more came to the quarantine tepees overnight as Hunting Owl made his rounds throughout the village. One of the three was an elderly man who lost his fight as the sun came up. Before breakfast, five more came, and Hunting Owl added a third tepee to the quarantine area.

Hunting Owl looked exhausted, and Desert Rose was sure she didn't look any better. Nonetheless, she sent him to his tepee to rest while she continued to care for the sick. The first glimmer of hope came mid-morning, when Prowling Bear's fever finally broke. Desert Rose could have shouted for joy, but her people might think it was meant as a funeral dirge.

Chapter 19
Help Arrives

Buck was finally on his way to the village. He had arrived home in the late afternoon two days before. Influenza was still working its way through Prairie Hills, so James went to find Dr. Mason. When he arrived at the ranch, they all sat around the fireplace in the ranch house as Buck explained what was happening in Julie's Kiowa village.

"Buck, I just received a shipment of medicine and am happy to send some with you, but I have several patients here that I cannot leave. If James can spare two of you, I suggest you take Luke with you. Julie is going to need help, especially if the influenza spreads throughout the village, as I suspect it might. Luke can treat influenza as well as I, and I want you to keep your distance from those who are ill."

Buck addressed his older brother, "May I take Luke?"

James looked over at Luke as he replied, "As long as it's all right with Luke, I can spare you both for a few days."

"Sure, I'll ride with you," Luke answered. "I'll need someone to translate for me, though."

"You'll have me and Julie. She's fluent in Kiowa, too."

"Right. I should have known that," Luke responded with a smile.

Buck informed him, "We'll leave at first light."

First light the next morning displayed a deep red sky. Buck stared at the ominous sign in the heavens, wanting to wish it away. He knew better. A big storm was coming. The ride would have to wait. While he might be tempted to go anyway, he wouldn't risk Luke's safety.

The storm did come, and it settled in and lasted all day. Buck took the opportunity to sit with Luke in front of the fire and teach him about Kiowa customs so Luke would know what to expect and how to act. When the storm finally passed and the temperature dropped, he instructed Luke, "Dress warmly tomorrow, and pack an extra blanket."

The entire ranch was still sleeping when Buck and Luke rode out together. When they stopped for a brief meal, Luke confided, "I hope I don't accidentally offend anyone by doing the wrong thing."

"Because you do not look Kiowa, they will not expect you to act Kiowa; however, respecting their customs will give you honor in their eyes. Do not fear, my brother, Julie and I will be there to guide you. Though if you call her Julie," Buck added with a smile, "she might not remember to answer. She is known as Desert Rose in the village, and I am known as Running Buck."

When Running Buck and Luke arrived at the village a couple of hours later, no one was on guard to greet them. They unsaddled the horses, releasing them in the corral. Luke removed the medicine bottles from his saddlebag, tucked them in his coat, and followed Running Buck into the heart of the village. No one was in sight.

Running Buck stopped in front of a tepee and spoke in Kiowa, *"Runs Like the Wind, it is Running Buck. Are you well?"*

Soon, the face of a middle-aged Indian woman appeared, *"Running Buck, I am glad you are back. Runs Like the Wind joined Prowling Bear in the tepee for the sick not long after you left. There are now three tepees for the sick, and Desert Rose hasn't slept since you left, caring for everyone from sunrise to sunrise."*

"Where are the tepees for the sick?" Running Buck wanted to know.

"The last three on this row." She pointed to the far end of the village.

"Many thanks. White Feather, this is my brother Luke. He is here to help Desert Rose care for our people."

"Welcome, Friend."

Luke had the feeling that he was being introduced, but he couldn't understand a word. Buck finally explained, "This is White Feather, the Kiowa mother of Desert Rose. She welcomes you."

"Thank you." Luke responded.

Running Buck translated, *"Many thanks."* To Luke he said, "Follow me."

Running Buck led him to the quarantine area and stopped. He spoke his wife's name, *"Desert Rose."* A moment later, they heard a sound from the second tepee as Desert Rose washed her hands and exited to stand face to face with the one she loved. She was visibly weak and utterly exhausted. When she met his gaze, tears fell from her eyes.

"How long has it been since you have slept?"

"Since the night we shared my narrow bed."

"You must rest. Luke is here to care for the sick so you can sleep. Tell him what he needs to know."

"How will he speak to them without me?" Desert Rose asked.

"I will translate for him," Running Buck answered.

"But you cannot go into the tepees and risk becoming ill."

Running Buck spoke gently but firmly, "My actions are not up for debate. You may relieve me after you have had a good sleep. Now, tell Luke what he needs to know."

She looked over at Luke, "Thank you for coming, Luke."

He nodded, prepared to listen intently to her words.

"This morning there were fourteen in the tepees of the sick, but seven more have come, bringing the number of the sick to twenty-one. We have added a fourth tepee to the quarantine area." She pointed to the tepee closest to her. "In the first tepee are three warriors. Prowling Bear was our first patient. His fever finally broke this morning. My father, Runs Like the Wind, and the Chief's son Gray Wolf are both stable and still strong." She swept her hand to the other tepees. "All of the others are still fighting. So far, we have lost two elderly villagers, and Morning Star lost her baby, Coyote." She saw the anguish in Running Buck's eyes, and her tears fell harder. She spoke again to Luke. "Coyote is in the little lidded basket just inside this tepee. He is the son of Gray Wolf, but do not tell him he is there with him. The baby should be with his mother until burial, but she did not want to spread the influenza to her other son."

"Hunting Owl is the medicine man, but I sent him to his tepee this morning to sleep. When he returns, he will visit the tepees in the village to be sure everyone is well and will bring any ill to you. The hand washing buckets are just inside each tepee, and everyone has their own cup and cooling cloth. Is there anything else you want to know?" Desert Rose's exhaustion and the emotions of the last two days were catching up with her fast.

"No, you go get some sleep," Luke ordered.

Buck spoke to his brother, "I will soon return."

His gaze had not left his wife's face, so he saw her face go pale. He lifted her in his arms just as she began to crumple to the ground and carried her to the tepee of White Feather. He laid her gently on her bed and covered her with the fur blanket. Her eyes fluttered open to meet his gaze. Buck whispered, "My Love, you have showed the courage and strength of ten warriors, but you must sleep now."

White Feather spoke from behind him, *"My face is turned. You may kiss her."*

Buck smiled, "She knows me well."

He leaned down and kissed his wife gently on the lips.

"Sleep well, my Love."

She was asleep before he reached the tepee flap on his way back to Luke.

Buck strode down the path to meet his brother. Luke was still standing where Buck had left him and asked as he approached, "Shall we begin our rounds?"

Buck nodded, "Come." He ducked into the first tepee, and Luke followed. Luke had never been inside of a tepee before and was surprised how spacious it really was. The air inside was comfortably warm and smelled of flowers and spice.

"Buck, where is the good smell coming from?"

"In the absence of white man's medicine, we use herbs, oils, and spices as medicine."

Buck took a whiff of the air.

"Desert Rose has used lavender, which relaxes and promotes sleep, and clove, which cleans sickness from the air."

Luke started his rounds to the left and knelt next to the first man, who looked from him to Running Buck behind him.

Running Buck spoke, *"Runs Like the Wind, this is Luke, our brother from the ranch. He has come to help Desert Rose care for the sick and has brought medicine."*

Luke pulled off his winter gloves and began his assessment.

As he felt the man's fevered skin and checked his heart rate, Luke heard Buck speak behind him, "This is Runs Like the Wind, the Kiowa father of Desert Rose."

Luke nodded and spoke to Desert Rose's father, while Running Buck continued to translate the conversation.

"It is a pleasure to meet you, but I wish the circumstances were different. How are you feeling this afternoon?"

"My headache has lessened somewhat, but my entire body still aches."

"Have you been able to keep down the water and broth?"

"Yes."

"Good. I am going to stir some medicine into your water cup that will help your fever and your aches. You are still strong, and I am hopeful your fever will break soon."

Luke refreshed the cloth on his face with the cool water and stirred the medicine in his cup before handing it to him. Runs Like the Wind was able to prop himself up and take the cup from Luke.

Luke stood and washed his hands before repeating the process with each of Desert Rose's patients. Prowling Bear was definitely on the mend, and Luke fully expected the fevers of Runs Like the Wind and Gray Wolf to break before nightfall. The ones in the other tepees were weaker and battling harder, but Luke hoped the medicine would help them in their fight.

Hunting Owl returned when Luke was rounding for the second time. Running Buck introduced them, then Hunting Owl resumed visiting the tepees outside the quarantined area looking for any others who were becoming ill.

The fevers of Runs Like the Wind and Gray Wolf did break as the sun slipped below the horizon. Though Prowling Bear was still cycling through fevers and sweats, he was strong enough to sit on the side of the bed for a little while and eat some buttered bread. Only two more sick were brought to Luke through the night.

News spread quickly that help and medicine had arrived. The tension in the village lessened. When the dawn of the new day arrived, some were starting to venture out of their tepees. Now the challenge would be to convince the people that the danger was not yet over.

Desert Rose arrived, looking much more rested, and joined Luke, sending Running Buck to help Hunting Owl in his quest to keep the well in their family tepees. She was overjoyed to learn that all three men in the first tepee were finally on the mend. The three regained their strength and could do more for themselves, and Luke and Desert Rose spent more of their time with those in the other tepees. Four more fevers broke that day, but two elderly men and one little girl still clung precariously to life. The next morning, one of the elderly lost his fight, but the other elderly man and the girl lasted until evening before finally succumbing to influenza.

Luke and Desert Rose worked together then in shifts so they could both get some rest. Running Buck stayed with Luke to translate when his wife was sleeping. Ever so slowly, the caregivers felt the tide of influenza turn. Fevers were breaking, strength was returning, and the three men in the first tepee were cleared to go home. Desert Rose secretly brought the lidded basket back to Morning Song. Only one more joined the tepees of the sick that day.

They still had sixteen villagers to care for, but the mood was lighter and more hopeful even in the tepees of the sick. Every one of their remaining patients seemed to be improving, though some were still waiting for their first fever to break.

Running Buck had returned from his tour of the well tepees and was translating for Luke for a bit while Desert Rose cleaned and aired out Prowling Bear's tepee. When she finished, she slipped into the second tepee, but what she saw gripped her heart in fear. Buck was standing behind Luke as he assessed and cared for his patient. Buck swayed slightly and unconsciously raised his hand to rub his forehead. For the first time since she had known him, he had not noticed her enter. She knew before she ever felt his face that her worst fear had been realized. Buck had influenza.

When she moved around to face Buck, the movement caught Luke's eye, and he glanced up at her. Seeing the concerned look on her face, he followed her gaze to Buck and realized what she saw.

She reached a practiced hand to his forehead, and breathed, "Oh, Buck, you're burning up."

Luke rose, washed his hands, and stood before his brother.

"We need to find a place for you to lie down." He asked Desert Rose, "Is the tepee of Prowling Bear still available?"

"Yes."

"Come with me," Luke instructed.

The simple movement of bending down to exit the teepee made Buck's head pound that much more. He was getting so woozy he could barely walk.

Desert Rose pleaded, "Luke, please help him." Luke turned to see Buck stagger, and he quickly went to him and grasped Buck's arm, pulling it around his shoulders to help Buck walk to the next tepee. Buck's legs began to buckle as he reached the bed where Runs Like the Wind had been a short time before. When Luke helped him lie down, Buck couldn't help the groan that escaped his lips.

Desert Rose brought in a clean cup, a bucket of drinking water, and a bowl with a cooling cloth and set them by her husband's bed. Luke finished assessing Buck and looked at Desert Rose, who was gazing at Buck. Tears were on her cheeks.

"Buck's fever and heart rate are high, but I think he'll be all right as long as they don't go higher."

Luke handed her the medicine bottle. "Stay with him and give him his evening dose of medicine. If there is any change, call for me. I will care for the others so you can care for Buck."

"Thank you, Luke."

Luke placed a brotherly hand on her shoulder. "Buck is strong. He will fight hard for you."

"His body is also very tired, with the immunity of the Kiowa. He was so busy protecting us that I neglected to protect him."

"Now you will give him the best care he could receive. I will be back later to check on you."

Luke slipped through the tepee door, and Desert Rose was alone with Running Buck.

As she bathed the face and neck of the one she loved, she prayed through her tears, "My Dear Father, I am afraid. Doc's words from weeks ago keep playing in my mind, 'If Buck were to get influenza, he would battle for his life.' Here we are now, Lord."

Desert Rose's lips quivered as she stifled another sob. She continued in prayer, "His strong body has been made weak because he spent his strength for me. Give him Your strength."

Her heart was so overwhelmed that she struggled to find the words. "This is a battle he must fight and win, or my heart will be forever broken. Please use whatever immunity Buck received from his white father to overcome what his body is lacking from his Kiowa family."

She pleaded, "Father, I love him so much. Please do not take him from me. Give me wisdom as I care for him. You are the Great Physician. Heal Buck, I pray. In the name of my Savior, Amen."

While Desert Rose was praying, Running Buck had fallen asleep. She leaned forward and gently kissed his forehead, his skin hot against her lips. After she massaged some lavender oil into the skin on his upper chest, she bathed his face again with cool water and draped the cloth across his forehead.

The time ticked by slowly as Desert Rose sat on the edge of Buck's bed watching him fitfully sleep. She knew the time would pass more quickly if she were busy helping Luke, but she couldn't leave Buck. Her place was right here. After sunset, Buck finally woke enough to sip some of the medicine-infused water. By that time, he was so weak that Desert Rose had to cradle his head and lift it for him.

Sometime in the middle of the night, Desert Rose suddenly woke from where she rested at Buck's bedside. Buck was thrashing in the bed. His fever had soared. She needed Luke now. She ran from the tepee and searched in the other tepees of the sick. In the last one she found Hunting Owl.

"Where is Luke?"

"Luke? Oh, you mean Eyes Like the Sky. He is sleeping in the tepee of Runs Like the Wind."

She would have smiled at Luke's new name if she weren't so full of dread and panic.

"Many thanks."

Desert Rose bolted from the tepee and ran to her childhood home. She entered quickly without the customary

214

greeting and went straight to Luke. Shaking his shoulder, she pleaded, "Luke, please wake up. I need you."

Luke was instantly awake. "What's wrong?"

She didn't take time to explain. "Please come now."

Luke immediately got up and followed her out of the tepee. As soon as her feet crossed the threshold, she sprinted to the tepee where Buck lay. Luke was right on her heels as she arrived.

Luke laid a hand on Buck's skin. "This is exactly what happened to you. We've got to get him cooled down now. I'm guessing we don't have the luxury of a big tub and a block of ice, do we?"

"No, but we do have the night air."

"Good thinking." Luke opened the tepee flap and secured it. A gust of chilly air entered the buffalo skin room. "Now, if I can get him to a sitting position, do you think you could pull off his tunic? We need to get more of his skin exposed to this cold air."

"Yes. I'll help you."

They worked together to remove Buck's tunic and lay him back down.

Luke instructed, "Wipe his skin with the cool water. When the cold air hits it, it may just feel like ice. Get his hair wet, too. That will cool off his head."

Desert Rose reached for the wet cloth and dampened his skin and hair.

"Now what?'

"We wait. Brrr. That air is cold. Buck's fever should start coming down soon. When it does, we need to be aware of any signs of shivering. That will be our cue to close the tepee door."

Desert Rose waited with bated breath. In a few minutes, the thrashing stopped, and Buck gradually looked more relaxed. She hesitantly reached out to touch his forehead, but breathed a sigh of relief when it was actually cooler.

"Luke, I think it's working."

Buck moaned and lifted a shaky hand to his forehead. Desert Rose asked, "My Love, are you still with me?"

Buck slowly turned his head toward his wife and answered softly with a scratchy voice, "Always and forever, My Love."

Desert Rose wept tears of relief. She knew the danger was far from over, but at least this one hurdle had been crossed.

By sunrise, his fever had spiked again. They worked to cool him down, but the high fever persisted longer before coming down a bit. Because he was now unable to keep even the smallest amount of water down, there was nothing Desert Rose could do to reverse his dehydration. She felt so helpless. If only his fever would break!

Luke left to relieve Hunting Owl and resume his rounds on the other ill villagers. Four more were cleared to return to their families. Only three more patients were waiting for their fevers to break. The epidemic was almost over. When Hunting Owl returned from his rest just after noon, Luke returned to Running Buck.

Though Luke had hoped to see improvement, Buck was starting to lose his fight. If not for the subtle movement of his chest as he breathed, Buck looked lifeless. Desert Rose was still tending to him, but Luke saw the fear in her eyes.

When Desert Rose slipped out of the tepee for a moment, Buck summoned all the strength he possessed to speak, "Luke . . . if our Great Spirit calls me Home . . . promise me you will take care of Julie . . . She is expecting our second baby . . . Raise him as your own."

Luke looked as if he were going to protest the need for such a promise, but Buck repeated, "Promise me."

Luke fought the tears that filled his eyes.

"I promise."

Buck gave the slightest of nods.

Luke spoke with a quiet intensity, "Buck, I have admired you and sought to be like you since your first day on the ranch. I have never known you to quit anything you resolved to do. You cannot quit this fight. You are married to the sweetest girl in the world, one who loves you very much. She needs you. I need you. You cannot give up. You, my warrior brother, must fight."

Buck had no more strength to respond. He simply closed his eyes as a single tear slid down his cheek.

When Desert Rose approached the tepee, she heard Buck's voice and stopped to listen. She rested her hand on her still-flat belly. Even as he was dying, Buck protected her and cared for her and the little life within her. She set down the water bucket before she fell to her knees and sobbed. This is where Luke found her several minutes later.

When Desert Rose looked up into Luke's face, she saw the tears in his eyes.

"Is he . . .?" She couldn't voice the word she feared.

Luke shook his head. "No, he is still barely hanging on to life. I need you to touch him. Hold his hand. Caress his face. Speak your words of love. Every fiber of his being needs to remember whom he is fighting for. He loves you more than life itself. Perhaps your touch and the sound of your voice will give him strength."

Luke lifted the water bucket and extended his other hand to help Desert Rose to her feet. "Come."

Her shaking legs led her to Buck's bedside once more, and Desert Rose prayed, "Lord, please grant me the strength for this day. My heart is breaking, and it hurts so much."

She sat on the edge of his bed and laid her head on his chest. The heartbeat that had always been so strong and steady was weak and rapid.

She stifled another sob to speak, "Buck, you are my warrior, my protector, my husband, my Love. Please find somewhere within you the strength to fight a little while longer. I don't think I could live without you."

She took a deep breath, sat up, and lifted his hand in hers before she continued, "I had planned to surprise you about our baby at Christmas, but you already know the wonderful news. You never miss anything. We have created life together, you and I. You will be the best father. No child could be more blessed."

She could stop the tide of tears no longer. "Please don't die. I love you."

Luke sat on the bed on the opposite side of the tepee. He rested his elbows on his knees and buried his face in his hands. He silently entered the throne room of Heaven. "Lord, my heart is torn in two. My brother is dying. Unless You heal him, he will soon lose his battle with influenza. He has entrusted me with his most priceless treasure. I am honored to be allowed to open my heart to Julie and her baby and love them in Buck's place. You know my heart. You know I fell in love with Julie when she first came to the ranch but buried my feelings for her when Buck loved her. Only the most special girl would be good enough for Buck, one who would understand his Indian ways. Buck and Julie are perfect for each other. She would be so easy to love, but her heart belongs to Buck. I would gladly bury my feelings again to see her joy return. Please let him live. Please, Father, let him live."

Desert Rose suddenly pleaded, "Buck, no! Don't leave me! Please don't die. Please, please." Her voice got softer and dissolved to tears as she hugged his hand to her cheek.

Luke rose and walked with heavy steps to his brother. He placed his hand on Buck's chest and felt Buck's heart as it beat slower and slower. Finally, it beat its last and went silent.

"No, Buck, you were supposed to fight for Julie, for your baby." Luke fell to his knees, no longer able to hold back the tears that had been threatening to fall.

From beside him, he heard Desert Rose speak softly through her tears, "Buck, I will love you always and forever."

They cried for many minutes before Desert Rose finally spoke again, "I will ask Hunting Owl for a burial shroud."

She rose to go, and Luke rose with her and wiped his eyes on his shirtsleeve.

"Julie." As Luke spoke her name, she looked at his tear-streaked face and began to cry again. Luke took one step to close the gap between them and wrapped his arms around her. In the fog of her grief, she suddenly realized that Buck had left her in the care of someone who truly loved her. The minutes passed, but she remained in Luke's comforting embrace, drawing strength from him, crying against his chest as he held her close.

Finally, she said, "I must get the burial shroud."

"I will go with you."

"No, it is the custom that the wife asks alone." She took a shaky breath. "I will return soon. The family helps with wrapping the body. Will you help me wrap him?"

Luke nodded, "Of course, I would be honored."

Desert Rose exited the tepee in search of Hunting Owl. She did not speak to anyone who passed her, for she couldn't trust her voice. She did not need to say anything. The tears of anguish on her face spoke volumes.

She found Hunting Owl in the third tepee for the sick and asked, "May I please have a burial shroud for Running Buck? He has been called to his meeting with the One True Great Spirit." Hunting Owl's face filled with sorrow. He nodded and left to retrieve it from his tepee.

Several minutes later, he returned with the leather shroud. She took it from him and walked silently back to where her husband lay. Luke was there to help her wrap his lifeless form. Desert Rose lifted Buck's left hand and kissed it.

As she gently removed his wedding ring, she repeated part of their wedding vows, "With you, I wish to be one until the bonds of death separate us." A fresh set of tears shook her frame.

When they had tied the last leather cord to hold the shroud closed, Desert Rose spoke, "We must tell White Feather and Runs Like the Wind." Luke walked with her to the home of her youth.

Desert Rose was about to enter the tepee, when she saw something that made her groan. Luke wrinkled his brow in concern. "What is it?" He followed her into the tepee.

"My husband has just died. Now the warriors are leaving gifts for me."

"What does that mean?" Luke asked.

"So far, three warriors have now asked me to be their wife."

Luke was stunned, "But they can't. I'm going to marry you."

Julie stared at him.

"That is, I want you to be my wife. Buck had me promise to care for you and your baby, but even if he hadn't asked me, I would want to do so. I have cared about you for a long time, but my thoughts were buried deep when Buck fell in love with you. I was content seeing the two of you so happy together. But now," Luke remembered Buck's lifeless face and tears filled his eyes once again, "Now I have lost my brother that I loved very much. Do not ask me to lose you, too. I love you and promise to love your little one as my very own."

Luke smoothly descended to one knee and reached for her hand. "Julie, will you marry me?"

Julie looked deeply into Luke's blue eyes and saw both agony and love there. This day had seemed like a nightmare, yet here was love and comfort in the midst of pain. She just didn't think it was fair to Luke, when her grieving heart still loved Buck so much. "Luke, I . . ."

"Please say yes," he pleaded. "I know your heart still belongs to Buck. When, in time, you are ready to open your heart to love another, I want to be the one who is there with you. Until then, I want to be the one to love and comfort you. Please say yes," he repeated.

How could she refuse the offering of such unselfish love, when she needed it so desperately?

"Yes."

Luke rose. He kissed her forehead and hugged her, holding her snugly against his chest. "Thank you."

After a few minutes had passed, Luke asked, "How do you refuse the other proposals?"

Desert Rose answered, "You must request an audience with the Chief to declare that Running Buck appointed you my protector and that you wish to marry me to preserve his honor."

"What if he refuses?"

"Because I am not of Kiowa blood, he should have no grounds to refuse you. But he is Chief, and his rulings are sometimes unpredictable. If he should refuse your request, tell him that Running Buck asked you to raise his son as your own. The care of a warrior's son is paramount in our culture, and Running Buck's wishes for his son would be honored."

"How do you know you are carrying a boy?"

"I don't, but here, all unborn babies are considered to be sons until proven otherwise at birth."

Luke nodded, "All right, how do I request an audience with the Chief?"

"We must ask Runs Like the Wind to speak to him on your behalf. You will be summoned when the Chief is ready."

Just then, Runs Like the Wind entered the tepee. Luke asked Desert Rose, "Will you translate for me?" When she nodded, he stood before her father. "The soul of Running Buck is now in Heaven with his Savior."

Runs Like the Wind nodded, for he already knew.

"I gave Running Buck my word that I would take care of his wife and his son. Now I ask you for your permission and your blessing to marry your daughter and protect Running Buck's honor."

Runs Like the Wind looked at his daughter, *"Are you with child?"*

"Yes."

"At last, a small glimmer of joy on such a day of mourning. Is Eyes Like the Sky a man of honor?"

"Oh, yes. He greatly admired Running Buck and is much like him in many ways. He will guide me in the ways of the One True Great Spirit and will love our child as his own."

"Then tell him he has my blessing." She gave Luke her father's message, and Luke nodded his thanks.

"May I request an audience with the Chief for his permission?" Luke ventured.

"*Yes, but Desert Rose would not be permitted at the meeting, and you would have no one to translate for you. There is an easier way. Have Desert Rose meet you here at the tepee at sunset, and all will see who she has chosen.*"

Luke turned to look at Desert Rose while she translated. "The expression on your face tells me this is more important than a simple meeting."

"Yes, this custom is how the Kiowa marry, how Buck and I were married after we left all of you at the ranch house." Her chin started to quiver as she remembered her wedding day. "The warrior stands before the tepee door, and the maiden comes to him at sunset and officially accepts his gift. He leads her into the tepee, and they become one."

"I have no gift to give you," Luke suddenly realized.

"You have given me your heart. It is enough. For Buck's honor and for yours, give me this when we meet." She slipped her wedding ring from her finger and handed it to Luke. "It has not left my finger since the day Buck put it on." Once again, her tears began to fall. "Luke, when we enter the tepee tonight, I don't think that I . . ."

"Nor would I expect that from you. Tonight is about protecting your honor and that of Buck and your family. Becoming one will be a time of great joy; it has no place on a day of great sorrow."

"Thank you, Luke."

Luke looked up to the sky. So much had happened on this day, but the time was only mid-afternoon. "I should go and help Hunting Owl in the tepees of the sick until the time of our wedding."

"Go. I will follow after you and help also."

When Luke left, Runs Like the Wind hugged his daughter. "*I am broken-hearted over the pain you have suffered today, but I am thankful that our Great Spirit has already provided you another*

223

husband who loves you. Many maidens live a lifetime without such a man, and God has given you two. You are blessed, my daughter."

Desert Rose left and made her way to the tepees of the sick. When she approached the tepee where Running Buck lay, she was drawn to his side. Again her tears began to flow. She had cried so many tears today, but she had to speak to her Love once more. She gazed at the shroud and imagined the smiling face of the one who still held her heart.

"Buck, I am going to marry Luke at sunset. I know we have your blessing because our marriage was your desire. My heart is broken and overwhelmed with grief, but I accepted him because I trust you. Because you chose him to be my husband, I will give your ring to Luke tonight."

She fell to her knees and reached out to rest her hand on his lifeless form, "Oh, my Love, I miss you so much. I will learn to open my heart to love Luke, but part of my heart will belong to you, always and forever." When the tide of her tears had abated, she rose and spoke one last time, "Goodbye, my Love." She exited to face what the future held, leaving part of her heart in the tepee with the man in the burial shroud.

Desert Rose entered the tepees of the sick to help Luke and Hunting Owl. The final stubborn fevers had broken, and the sick were healing. The epidemic was over. She and Luke were no longer needed here. She wanted to go home.

After a time, Hunting Owl looked heavenward and said, *"The sun hangs low in the sky. Remind Eyes Like the Sky to go."*

Knowing that they had the blessing of this wise Kiowa elder, she reminded Luke, "Sunset is near. You should go. Stand in front of my family's tepee. I will come to you when the sky is painted."

Luke met her gaze and nodded, "I will await your coming." Desert Rose looked on him with new eyes as she watched him exit the tepee and walk down the path to her parents' buffalo skin home. This handsome man loved her. He was tall and strong, but gentle and kind. Even with the weight of his own grief, his shoulders were strong enough to bear the burden of her grief, too.

While the sun continued to sink to the horizon, Desert Rose prayed, "Please help me to become the best wife I can be for Luke. Heal my heart so I can love him as he should be loved."

The sun finally dipped below the horizon, and the colors grew in the sky. To her heart, the setting sun represented the death of the one she loved, and the painted sky was a sign of hope. As she made her way down the familiar path, she passed several warriors waiting by their tepees, but she found Luke's gaze and never looked away.

She stood before him and spoke first in Kiowa, *"Desert Rose accepts the gift from Eyes Like the Sky,"* then she repeated the words in English.

At the look of surprise on Luke's face, she asked, "Did you not know that you had been gifted with a Kiowa name?"

"No. Who named me?"

"I don't know for sure, but Hunting Owl is usually the giver of names. He was the one who named me when I came to live here. Your name suits you."

"May I return your ring to you now?"

When she nodded, he pulled the ring from his pocket and lifted her left hand. "This ring has been a symbol of unconditional love. That love will not change. Only the giver of that love has changed." He slipped her ring on her finger.

Julie held Buck's wedding ring in her other hand. When she opened her hand, a quiet breath of surprise escaped from Luke's lips. "This ring belonged to a man that I love very much. Now I give it to you, with the promise that one day I will love you just as much. This ring was worn by my husband, my warrior, the Chief of my home, my Love. With Buck's blessing, those titles are now transferred to you." She lifted Luke's left hand and slid the ring onto his finger. It was a perfect fit.

"I am honored to wear Buck's ring."

Julie needed him to understand, "It is no longer Buck's ring. It is yours, as I am now yours."

The colors of the sunset were beginning to darken into nightfall.

"Come." Luke reached for her hand and ducked into the tepee with Julie following him. After the flap of buffalo skin closed behind them, Luke faced Julie and held both of her hands in his.

"May I say my vow to you before God?"

Julie looked into his blue eyes and nodded.

He spoke softly and reverently, "I, Luke Matthew Hamilton, choose you, Julie Suzanne Peterson Matthews, to be my wife. You and you alone are the one I wish to love, to cherish, to honor, to protect, to provide for until death separates us. As the head of our home, I will guide you in the ways of the True God. I give you my name and my heart. I am completely yours. I love you, Mrs. Hamilton."

Julie took a shaky breath and spoke her vow, "I, Julie Suzanne Peterson Matthews, choose you, Luke Matthew Hamilton, to be my husband. I will honor and obey you as the head of our home." She paused, and her tear-filled eyes overflowed. "I cannot truthfully say that I am completely yours, because I don't know if I will ever be complete again, but I am yours, broken pieces and all. I am sorry I do not have more to give you on our wedding day."

"I will ask nothing of you. When you are ready, I will be here."

Luke pulled her into his embrace. Here she found strength, comfort, and love. Buck was right. She needed Luke.

When Julie's tears finally stopped, Luke whispered, "You are exhausted. You must rest before we ride home tomorrow."

Julie nodded. She took two steps toward the larger bed that had been adorned with sprigs of lavender when she realized that Luke was walking away from her toward her narrow bed.

"Luke?"

He turned and met her gaze. She requested, "Please, sleep close to me tonight."

He crossed the room and slipped under the blanket of the larger bed and lifted the edge of the blanket for Julie to crawl in. She curled up on her side with her back against Luke's chest.

He wrapped his arm around her and whispered in her ear, "Rest well, my Wife. I love you." Those stubborn tears came again and dampened her pillow, but the combination of the lavender and Luke's closeness helped her relax into a deep restful sleep.

When Julie awoke the next morning, the events of the day before seemed like a terrible dream. The air was crisp and smelled of lavender. The sun was bright and inviting. The day felt fresh and new and full of promise. As she blinked off the fog of deep sleep and looked at the hand holding hers, she saw fair skin, not the bronze skin of the Kiowa. Luke. The terrible dream had not been a dream. Like a great tidal wave, the sorrow and pain of yesterday swept over her heart and washed away her joy. For Luke's sake, she must find her joy again.

Luke felt her stir and whispered, "Are you awake, My Love?"

She sniffed through fresh tears, "Buck always called me that."

Not wanting to do anything to cause her more pain, Luke asked softly, "Would you rather I didn't?"

"No, I find comfort in hearing it . . . Luke?"

"Yes?"

"Thank you for loving me."

He propped up his head with his elbow. "I am honored to be allowed to love you," Luke replied. "Are you ready to go home?"

"Yes. I must say goodbye to my parents and my best friend Morning Song. I do dread having to relive these last few days to tell our family what has happened."

Luke nodded. "I will saddle the horses. Would you ask Runs Like the Wind to help me lift Buck onto Wind Dancing? His horse should be the one to carry him to his final resting place."

He leaned over and kissed Julie on her forehead. "This day will not be easy, but I will be with you, loving you every minute."

Luke pulled on his boots and walked to the corral. Julie rose and made the bed before going out to find her parents and Morning Song.

After her father and Luke secured Running Buck's shrouded body on Wind Dancing, the Chief came, *"Desert Rose, stand before me."*

She walked over to the Chief while Luke watched.

"Look at me."

Desert Rose lifted her respectfully downcast eyes.

"You have shown the courage of many warriors. On behalf of our village, I wish to thank you for caring for our people. Our hearts break with yours over the passing of your warrior to the land of the Great Spirit. After your time of grieving, may you and Eyes Like the Sky know much joy and have many sons."

"Many thanks, Chief Soaring Eagle."

Luke could not understand what was said, but when he glanced over at Runs Like the Wind, Desert Rose's father looked at him with smiling eyes. The Chief turned to go, and Desert Rose returned to Wind Dancing and her family.

` Runs Like the Wind placed a fatherly hand on her shoulder, *"I am proud of you, my Daughter. You have brought great honor to our family."*

She translated for Luke, who quietly added, "These people needed you, and you gave everything you had to help them. Everything. You deserved the Chief's blessing."

White Feather approached them, *"You must eat before you leave."*

Desert Rose was quick to reply, *"I am not hungry."*

"Perhaps not, but you must feed Running Buck's son. Come." Her mother was not going to let her refuse, so she followed her dutifully to the cooking fire and ate what she was given.

White Feather and Runs Like the Wind brought Desert Rose and Eyes Like the Sky into their tent for hugs and final goodbyes. The trip home seemed to take forever, partly because Luke was riding more slowly so Wind Dancing would not lose his burden, and partly because they were both dreading the emotions they would face when they arrived home.

Chapter 20
Heavy Hearts

James was the first one to spot Luke and Julie from the north pasture when they entered the ranch early that evening. As he approached them on horseback, he took in the scene before him in disbelief. His gaze was drawn to the shrouded form lying across Wind Dancing.

"Please tell me that is not Buck."

The tears streaming down Julie's face gave him the answer he did not want to know.

His eyes filled with sudden tears as he addressed Luke, "What happened?"

Luke's voice cracked with emotion as he tried to hold back his tears. "If you don't mind, could you get everyone together at the ranch house so we can tell all of you at once?"

James nodded in understanding, "Of course."

He rode ahead to gather his family. They were all waiting for Luke and Julie when they arrived. Emma was crying openly. James was weeping quietly, and the other boys wore expressions of utter shock.

When Luke and Julie had dismounted, he reached for her hand and led her into the ranch house, where they sat on the sofa in front of the fire to warm up. The rest of the family came in and sat around them. Several minutes passed before Luke could find his voice. He described the epidemic conditions he and Buck encountered when they arrived to the village. He told them of Julie's courage and utter exhaustion after single-handedly organizing the village into quarantined areas and caring for all of the sick. Luke explained how Buck had insisted on translating for him in the tepees of the sick so Julie could sleep. When he began the story of Buck contracting influenza, he buried his face in his hands and wept. That was when Emma silently noticed the ring on Luke's left hand. Luke eventually regained his composure enough to continue the story, describing Buck's last hours on earth, including his promise to Buck to take care of Julie.

Emma pointed to Luke's hand and asked simply, "Are you married?"

"Yes, Julie became my wife last night." In response to the murmurs of surprise, he quickly explained, "The Indian culture does not allow time for grieving. Several warriors proposed to her yesterday. To preserve the honor of Buck and Julie's Kiowa family, we were married at sunset."

Luke took a deep breath and wiped his eyes.

He addressed his oldest brother, "If you could help me carry Buck's body into the barn, we can make a casket for him and bury him on the Hill next to his daughter tomorrow morning." All four brothers rose to help Luke.

Before Luke stood to join them, Julie whispered, "Thank you, Luke."

He lifted the hand that was in his and kissed it.

When Luke rose and exited the house with his brothers, Emma sat where Luke had been sitting and wrapped her arms around her niece. Julie's quiet tears turned to uncontrollable sobs as she clung to Emma.

The boys worked together for several hours to fashion the casket for their brother. By the time Luke returned to the ranch house, Julie had fallen asleep on the sofa. Emma sat in the chair, still weeping. She clutched a handkerchief near her cheek and looked up at Luke with puffy eyes.

Emma nodded as Luke whispered, "I'm going to take Julie home." He hated to risk waking her, but he knew she would want to go home. He carefully lifted Julie and carried her in his arms out of the house, down the river trail, and to her home - their home. He ducked through the tepee entrance and laid Julie gently on the bed. After he tucked her in under the fur blanket, he stood beside the bed for a while and just watched her sleep. Yes, his heart was grieving, but amidst the pain of loss there was new hope. The sweetest girl in the world, the one he had secretly loved, was now his wife. If that weren't amazing enough, he was going to be a father in about seven months.

While he gazed at Julie's face, he agonized over her grief, "Lord, heal her broken heart, protect the life growing within her, and give me the wisdom to help her find joy again."

He crawled into the other side of the bed to sleep. When Julie woke up from a nightmare screaming Buck's name in the middle of the night, Luke was right there to comfort her and hold her in his arms.

The next morning, Julie woke to find Luke filling the tub with warm water. "What are you doing?"

"When I was growing up, my mom always said that nothing could soothe a woman's soul like a warm bath. I thought you might like to wash off some of the trail dust before . . . our walk to the Hill. I'll head to the bunkhouse to get cleaned up and give you some privacy."

When he left, she looked over at the tub. It did look inviting. As she sank into the warm water, she agreed with Luke's mom. She felt clean and relaxed after bathing with her handmade lavender soap. Once she finally brushed out all of the tangles in her hair, she washed her hair, too.

She changed into a dark green dress and was just putting the last few pins in her wet tresses when she heard Luke's voice, "Are you dressed?"

"Yes, Luke, come in." From her reflection in the mirror, she saw him enter the tepee and drop his dirty clothes in the corner basket.

"I feel like a new man; I must have had an inch of dirt on my skin." When he looked over at Julie, he stopped, speechless.

Julie turned to face him, "What is it?"

Luke whispered, "You are beautiful, my Love." He saw the hint of her smile before she dissolved into tears again.

"Will I never stop crying?"

"The tears help to heal your broken heart. Do not fight them." He stepped over to her and pulled her gently to his chest. When her tears stopped, he spoke again, still holding her close to himself, "Pastor Kendrick and Emily will be here at ten."

"What time is it now?" Julie wondered.

"About half past nine," Luke answered.

"Would you keep your arms around me until we need to go?" Julie asked quietly.

"I was hoping you would let me hold you awhile longer," he whispered.

After a few minutes, Julie commented, "I can't believe I slept in so late. You should have woken me."

"Grief is exhausting. You seemed to be resting so comfortably after the ordeal of your nightmare last night, that I wasn't about to wake you."

"What time did you get up?" Julie asked.

"Just after five. After I watched you sleep for a bit to make sure you were all right, I helped with barn chores and the digging of Buck's grave. Then I rode out to speak with Pastor Kendrick about Buck's burial. While I was there, I asked him what we needed to do to make our marriage legally binding. He's going to take care of the details today."

Julie gave a shaky smile, "And all I have done is take a bath. That makes me feel rather lazy. Thank you for thinking of the marriage license. That was a detail Buck and I included in our wedding, but you and I wouldn't have had that luxury even if I had had the presence of mind to remember."

"You are anything but lazy, my Love." Luke smiled a little, "As for the license, I need to make our marriage binding before you have the presence of mind to change your mind."

At this comment, Julie pulled away just enough to meet Luke's gaze. She saw the twinkle in his eyes and realized he was teasing her. She didn't exactly smile, but her expression brightened a bit. "I'm afraid you are stuck with me. Buck was right, you know. I need you. I am so thankful you were there for me. I'd have never made it through the last few days without you. Thank you for marrying me."

"I love you, Julie." He leaned forward and kissed her forehead. "The time has come for us to meet the family on the Hill." Julie took a deep breath, and her eyes filled with tears. "Come. Let us honor Buck together." As he released his embrace, he reached for her hand, and they walked quietly hand-in-hand to where the others had gathered.

When Emily hugged Julie, her tears overflowed once again. Julie approached the grave and discovered the wooden casket that held the body of her beloved was already neatly fitted in the ground. She clung to Luke's hand and rested her head against his shoulder as fresh tears streamed down her cheeks.

Pastor's words were brief but heartfelt. He, too, had lost a spouse, so he understood the grief firsthand. Everyone circled around Buck's grave was weeping. The dull ache around Julie's heart that had been numbed by her grief magnified now as she looked into Buck's grave. She turned and buried her face in Luke's shoulder as his four brothers covered the casket with dirt. When they finished, each of her family members filed by to give her a hug and descended the Hill toward the ranch house to gather together once more.

When everyone but Luke had gone, Julie dropped to her knees next to the freshly turned earth. "Buck, I know you are in heaven with our daughter and our Savior, not in the box beneath the ground in front of me. If there is a window from heaven, please tell our little girl how much I love her. I will always love you, but now I will open my heart to the brother you chose to be my husband and the father to our baby. Thank you for creating life with me and for loving me enough to give me Luke with your final words. I love you."

Julie stayed on her knees for several more minutes, weeping quiet tears. When she stirred to rise, Luke stepped forward and offered his hand to help her stand. He gently pulled her toward him and held her close. This is the view Emma witnessed as she looked up the Hill from her kitchen window.

Emma whispered to herself, "Luke really does love her. She is blessed more than she knows."

Julie and Luke joined their family as they sat around the kitchen table. Emma and Emily served lunch.

As Julie stared at her empty plate, Luke leaned in and whispered in her ear, "I know you're not at all hungry, but you should eat something for you and our little one."

Julie nodded. She had not missed the "our" in his statement. Something somewhere inside her tried to smile, but it never made it close to her face.

Later that afternoon, as Pastor Kendrick stood with Luke and Julie in the flower garden, James and Emily witnessed them renew their vows. Pastor concluded, "I now officially pronounce you to be what you already know to be true. You are husband and wife. Luke, you may kiss your bride."

As Luke lifted Julie's left hand to his lips and kissed it, he whispered, "I love you, Julie Hamilton." She lifted her gaze from her hand to meet his blue eyes. A solitary tear escaped down her cheek.

Pastor Kendrick asked, "When I inform our church family about what has happened in your lives this last week, is there anything special you want me to include?"

Luke seemed to read Julie's thoughts and replied, "Yes, I am going to be a father, but the new life within Julie was created by her and Buck. For Buck's honor and Julie's, I wish everyone to understand that she carries Buck's baby."

Pastor nodded his understanding. Luke looked up at James, whose eyes were glistening with unshed tears. Then he met the gaze of his wife, who whispered, "Thank you, Luke."

Luke nodded and said, "Let's go tell our family the good news. They need some joy today."

Chapter 21
Finding Joy

The next Sunday morning, while Luke helped his brothers with chores, Luke asked James, "Whose turn is it to hitch and drive the buggy?"

James thought a moment, "Actually, it's your turn."

"Perfect," Luke gave a little smile. He readied the buggy before he walked home to have breakfast with Julie. After they ate, they strolled hand-in-hand to the buggy parked in front of the ranch house. Without a word, Luke smoothly swept Julie up in his arms and set her gently on the buggy seat. This familiar kindness brought a shaky smile and quiet tears.

"Thank you, Luke." He smiled his acknowledgment and extended a hand for Emma to climb up. When they arrived at the church, Luke gave Emma a hand down, then reached for Julie's waist and lifted her down the way Buck always had. Once more, Luke showed her that he loved her. The church service that morning was very emotional for everyone, and Julie was so thankful Luke was there beside her.

Day by day, Julie fell into a comfortable routine. She would get up early with Luke and prepare breakfast while he did his morning chores. After breakfast, she would help Luke in the barn to stay busy and spend time with her new husband. She would make lunch for the brothers in the bunkhouse. After lunch, she would help Emma or take

Wind Dancing for a ride before returning home to make dinner for Luke. The numbness she had felt around her heart was gradually wearing off, but the dependable routine became a shield to protect her from unwanted emotions.

Emma silently watched the two of them. Julie was smiling more, especially when she was with Luke, but his interaction with her was more like a brother than a husband. As she studied Julie, she ascertained the reason. Being the Mom on this ranch, it was up to her to say something to Julie. One Saturday night in early December, Emma found an opportunity after a family dinner at the house.

"Julie, I'm concerned for you. Have you and Luke . . .?"

Julie shook her head no.

"That boy longs for you."

Emma's statement caught her off guard. "How do you know?"

"His eyes speak volumes when he looks at you."

"Why haven't I seen it?" she asked.

Emma answered, "Because he guards his gaze every time you look up at him. Find your joy, Julie. Open your heart to Luke. He loves you so much."

Julie became lost in thought as she searched her heart. When she considered her feelings for Luke, she was rather surprised to realize that she loved him, truly loved him, like a wife should love her husband. She had become too comfortable in her routine and had neglected to see how unfair their relationship was to Luke. He had given her his heart on the sunset they were married in the Kiowa village, and he had kept his promise to never ask anything more of her than she was ready to give.

She prayed silently as she glanced over where Luke was sitting with his brothers, "Lord, forgive me. You have given me a precious gift in Luke, and I have not been the wife I should have been these last two months. Give me the wisdom to know how to tell him the feelings of my heart."

Luke was facing slightly away from her, laughing at something James had just said. As Julie continued gazing at him unnoticed from the kitchen, she allowed herself to realize just how handsome he was. He was now just over six feet tall. He was thin, but muscular, with medium blond hair with just enough wave to feather perfectly and still look nice when it was tousled. He had a boyish face with an easy smile, but his eyes were his most striking feature. Luke's eyes were a bright crystal blue, with a dark blue ring around them. Though Luke was blond, his eyelashes and eyebrows were dark brown, framing his eyes and making them stand out that much more. His appearance could easily turn the head of any young lady, but he only had eyes for her. She was truly blessed.

The next morning, as Pastor was preaching on Job's wife, he commented, "Many of us give Job's wife a hard time for her despair and her harsh words to her husband. Do not forget that she, too, just lost all ten of her children, and she was watching her husband go through what seemed like torture. In her grief, she reacted just as most of us would, with utter broken-hearted desperation. When grief surrounds our hearts, many unintentionally hurt the ones closest to us, the ones we love the most."

As Julie pondered his words, they weighed heavily on her heart. Thanks to Emma's keen perception, she realized just whom she had hurt in her grief. Luke was sitting close on her right, with his open Bible in his right hand, and his left hand resting on his leg. Julie reached over and lifted his hand and held it above her lap. She stared at his wedding ring and fingered it thoughtfully. Luke, who had looked over at his wife when she moved his hand, now gently wrapped his fingers around her hand. When she glanced up at him with misty eyes, his eyes communicated his concern.

The service concluded, and Luke, Julie, and Emma had a quiet ride home. Luke wanted to be alone with Julie. When they arrived in front of the ranch house, Luke helped Emma down and spoke quietly, "Julie will be in to help you in a few minutes." Emma smiled a knowing smile and nodded.

Luke turned to help Julie. When her feet landed softly on the ground before him, he caught her gaze. "Take a walk with me."

"I'd love to, but Emma will need me in the kitchen."

"I told her you'd be there in a little bit." As Julie nodded, Luke took her hand in his and led her to the flower garden beside the house, the same garden where they had repeated their wedding vows two months prior. The sky was clear, and the sun was bright, giving the sensation of warmth though the temperature was chilly. The beautiful blossoms that had surrounded them with brilliant colors and sweet fragrances now lay dormant, awaiting the kiss of spring. Even still, this garden was a soothing place. When they were far enough around the house to be out of sight of the bunkhouse, Luke stopped and faced his wife. He pulled her against his chest and held her close. "When you were missing Buck during the church service, I so wanted to wrap you in my arms right then and there."

Julie clung to him, realizing yet again how blessed she was to have this man she didn't deserve. She replied softly, "I wasn't thinking of Buck; I was thinking about you."

"Me?" Luke crinkled his brow in a puzzled expression.

"Yes. I have been like Job's wife. While I have been consumed with my sorrow, I have hurt the one I care for the most. You have married a wife, but I have only given you a companion." Julie pulled away just enough so their eyes could meet. "Please forgive me, Luke."

Luke watched as a tear overflowed and dropped from her eyelashes, and he prayed for the wisdom to comfort her. He reached up and gently wiped away the tear with his thumb. "You are forgiven, my Love, though you have not done anything wrong." He paused, looking for the right words. "Let me remind you of something. In the Kiowa culture, the protection and provision of the women is dependent upon them being married. In the harsh conditions of nomadic life in the plains, the warriors honor the dead and show their care for the widows by ensuring they are not even a day without the security of marriage."

"Our culture is far different. Widows are expected to be given time to grieve. Months or even years are needed before a heart can heal enough to love again. You may have grown up Kiowa, but you married Buck for love, not honor. Your heart still held to the ideals of your white family."

"You and Buck were one in every way. When he died, part of you was ripped away, leaving a gaping wound in your heart. A wound of any kind must be carefully cared for to minimize the scar and prevent infection. A wounded heart is most delicate. Your heart is starting to heal, and you have been careful not to allow any bitterness to infect your soul. I have prayed often that my words would give comfort, but complete healing takes time. If the circumstances had been different, I would have honored your time to grieve."

"You would have waited?" Julie softly inquired.

"Yes. I would have made my intentions known, but I would have waited to propose." Luke smiled, "The Lord's plans, though, were far better than my own. If I had not married you on the evening of Buck's passing, I would never have been able to hold you and stay near you as I do. I am beyond amazed that you are mine. I am thankful every day that I am able to fall asleep and wake up next to the one I love."

"You are the most wonderful husband. No woman has ever been more loved."

Luke again pulled her in close and pondered her words silently, thinking that he heard the hint of an "I love you." Maybe someday soon she would be able to say those words aloud.

A few minutes passed until he released her. He looked into her warm brown eyes and reminded her, "I love you, Julie. I will always love you."

Julie smiled, "Thank you, Luke."

Luke led her around to the front of the house, where he held the door open for her. "I'll be in as soon as I unhitch the buckboard. Save me a seat." He winked at her, and she smiled into his twinkling blue eyes.

"I'll do my best, but you know how crowded the dinner table is." She heard Luke's laugh as she entered the house to help Emma. Her plan from the night before would have to be amended. Today would be the day.

Luke and Julie arrived at their home after Sunday dinner with the family, when Julie looked into his eyes and smiled. "I know Christmas is still two weeks away, but I really want to give my gift to you today. Would you mind an early present?"

Luke smiled, "I wouldn't mind."

"Stay right there." She lifted the lid of her cedar chest and removed a small white box adorned with a red bow. She handed the box to Luke, who wrinkled his brow in curiosity. "Open it."

He held the box in one hand and carefully lifted the lid to reveal a white piece of paper with two words written in neat script, "Kiss me."

He smiled, then swallowed hard and hesitated as he asked softly, "Are you sure? When my lips touch yours . . ."

Julie understood the deeper question he was asking her. She gazed into his eyes. "You, my husband, are so handsome. I want to get lost in your beautiful blue eyes and melt in your arms. I wish to be yours, completely yours. Luke, I love you." Suddenly it was there in his eyes, the look of longing he had been guarding from her.

Julie smiled at the man she loved as he looked again at the piece of paper in his box. His face lit up in the sweetest smile, and he set the box aside.

He took the step to close the gap between them and whispered, "Please say it again."

Julie's smile made her entire face glow.

"Luke, I love you."

Luke bent his head until his lips were only an inch from hers.

"I can't stop smiling. I love you so much." When their lips finally met, their first kiss was everything they had hoped for.

Epilogue

Five months later, a rather rotund Julie went into labor about two o'clock in the morning. The house that Luke and his brothers had started building for him and Julie in the clearing near the tepee wasn't quite finished yet, and the tepee was quite warm this time of year, even at night. For her comfort, Luke brought his wife to Emma's house for the delivery. Emma sent Tim for Dr. Mason, but he was delivering another baby at the Moore house. Tonight's full moon was making it a night for babies.

When Emma told Julie that Doc was detained, Julie was as calm as a woman in labor could be. "If he doesn't make it, Luke can deliver our baby."

"What? No, no. We'll wait for Doc," Luke insisted.

Julie laughed at her husband's flustered face. "You've delivered hundreds of babies, certainly enough to know they wait for no one."

"Delivering calves and foals is far different from delivering a baby, especially when the baby is your own."

"How different could it be?" Julie teased. Luke gave her a look that said he didn't want to find out.

Nevertheless, Luke and Emma stayed with Julie while the brothers congregated downstairs. Julie's contractions kept getting closer and more regular, but Doc still had not yet arrived. Luke was starting to get anxious, but when the baby's birth was imminent, Doc burst through the door. Luke breathed, "Thank you, Lord."

"Normally I throw the fathers out, but the baby is nearly here, and Julie needs someone to push against. Get up on the bed behind her and bend your knees so she has something to hold onto." Luke followed his instructions. "Julie, get ready to push." Julie nodded.

A few minutes later, a baby's robust cry filled the room.

"Julie, Luke, you have a son."

Luke whispered from behind her, "Julie, we have a son."

Emma slipped out of the room to call down the stairs, "It's a boy!"

The cheers from below brought a smile to Julie's face, even as tired as she was.

Emma asked, "Do you have a name picked out?"

Julie nodded, "Yes, he is Matthew Phillip Running Buck Hamilton. Matthew, the name that belongs to both of his fathers, means 'Gift of God,' and our son is definitely God's gift to us. The name Phillip means 'lover of horses,' and training horses was a passion Buck and I shared together."

"Such a big name for a little guy, but it's perfect," Emma commented. Doc and Emma cleaned him up and wrapped him in a small blanket before handing him to Julie.

Luke looked over Julie's shoulder from where he still sat behind her and reached around to touch his son. "He looks just like Buck must have looked as a baby, only his skin is a bit lighter."

Julie spoke in awe, "He's beautiful." Luke couldn't agree more.

As Emma looked on with a smile, she marveled at God's Sovereign plan. Julie had come home to this room. Julie had regained her sight in this room. Julie had also lost her first baby in this room. Now, she and Luke held new life in this very room. Emma thought about the tragedy Julie had endured and prayed that her future with Luke would be filled with God's blessings. Throughout her journey, Julie's faith in her Lord inspired those around her. Now, holding her baby with Luke's arms around them both, Julie had found her joy once again.

Acknowledgements

Putting this story into print is a dream come true for me. Those who helped make this book possible deserve my sincere gratitude.

First, I would like to thank the wonderful man who encouraged me to pursue publication of my story in the first place. My husband Bob has been my faithful supporter in this journey. He kept me laughing with his ridiculous plot line suggestions, but his one serious suggestion helped the story become what it is.

With the trepidation of a novice author, I sent my initial manuscript to Cindy Bower, my friend and sister-in-law. She has been my primary advisor throughout this process, from her initial thoughts, insightful feedback on each revision, and honest comments on the final steps of publication. Thank you for being with me each step of the way.

My dear friend Jennifer Ewoldt, DVM was an invaluable resource, for she is both a veterinarian and a cattle ranch owner. Her knowledge of animal husbandry was a huge blessing to this city girl.

Holly Talley used her expertise as an advanced composition teacher to edit my manuscript. The final copy is much improved because of her suggestions.

The photograph on the front cover is the portrait of Olivia Gideons, a soft-spoken young lady whose love for the Lord is evident in her life. She is never without a smile.

Thanks also belong to Sarah Horton, Rhonda McLaughlin, Sally Stevens, Pam Dewhurst, and Erica Skattebo who read my manuscript's early drafts and willingly shared their comments.

My boys, Will and Matthew, asked me to read my book to them as their bedtime story. They are already asking for book two.